Praise for *Tall Short Stories from the Mind of Garbo*

"Over the years, Chuck Hajinian has produced many wonderful short stories—oftentimes incorporating his remarkable collection of Armenian jokes and anecdotes. In addition to friends and acquaintances alike, new readers can now enjoy many of them in his entertaining new book – which I heartily recommend for its originality and color. I'm certainly eager to get my copy!"
  –Oscar S. Tatosian, Honorary Consul for the Republic of Armenia in Chicago

"Chuck has such a voice when he writes that is so relatable. I also find myself rereading lines that he's written because I just want to enjoy, again, the way he's described something or the way he worded it with his use of figurative language. I especially love reading the parts about the Armenian culture and his experience with it and understanding of it. He truly is so talented and has such a gift."
  –Virginia Oliva, English Teacher

"For the past decade, Chuck's dedication to SOAR's orphaned population is unparalleled, as evidenced by his earmarking to SOAR all profits from this book. What makes Chuck so captivating is knowing that something new is always around the corner. A dentist by training, Chuck enjoys stand-up comedy and putting his experiences and feelings to paper. The 41 pieces in *Tall Short Stories from the Mind of Garbo* offers a wonderful flavor of Armenian optimism. Witty, poignant, encouraging, and insightful, Chuck's stories give you a glimpse into how Armenians perceive the world, how humor offers a measure of peace in our daily lives, and how easy life can be if relationships were grounded in altruism, trust, and mutual respect."
  –George S. Yacoubian, Jr., Ph.D., LL.M., S.J.D., M.S., Founder of the Society for
  –Orphan Armenian Relief - SOAR

TALL SHORT STORIES
from the Mind of
GARBO

CALUMET EDITIONS

Minneapolis

First Edition September 2022
Tall Short Stories from the Mind of Garbo.
Copyright © 2022 by Chuck Hajinian.
All rights reserved.

No parts of this book may be used or reproduced by any means, graphic, electronic, or mechanical, including photocopying, recording, taping or by any information storage retrieval system, without the written permission of the publisher except in the case of brief quotations embodied in critical articles and reviews.

This is a work of fiction. All of the characters, names, incidents, organizations, and dialogue are either the products of the author's imagination or are used fictitiously.

Printed in the United States of America.
10 9 8 7 6 5 4 3 2 1

ISBN: 978-1-950743-94-0

Cover and book design by Gary Lindberg

TALL SHORT STORIES
from the Mind of
GARBO

Chuck "Garbo" Hajinian

Chuck "Garbo" Hajinian
#122

CALUMET EDITIONS
Minneapolis

Table of Contents

Praise from an Unbiased Expert 1
Introduction 3
Third-Grade Memory Held Captive 5
    My young heart beats for ice skates and a painted tiger
Pepper on your Caesar 11
    Distracted deep thoughts by a beauty
The Anatomy of a Kiss: Part 1 13
    A kiss, more important than food?
The Anatomy of a Kiss: Part 2 15
Ladies' Night at Revere's Bar 19
    Time stands still while it shows us a mirror
My Great-Grandma Catherine and Teddy Roosevelt 23
    Their hearts were one, though they never met
Quarantine #1 Observation 29
    A fish invades the awareness of French Impressionists
"A First Love" 31
    Connie, opposites in love revisited
The Night Before the Battle of Avarayr 35
    Conversations that never took place
    41
    Best borrowed jokes worth repeating
Tea for Two on the Putting Green of Life 45
    Sometimes words evaporate; where do they go?
A Hero for All of Us— Shavarsh Karapetyan 47
    A young man gives up his career to save twenty-one people
Breakfast with Claude Monet 1922 53
    Why do we wish they never left us

Quarantine Short Story #9: Listening to Distant Tambourines..55
    Pinkies in the air, dancing to the sounds of long ago
Chapter Eternal for Nazar Hajinian 59
    A journey of a deeper faith for my father
Double Vision Correction 69
    A child's crossed eyes sees with adult perception
Golfing with Dad Revisited 73
    Going golfing with Dad after he has passed
Summerfest in a Green Pinto 1978......................75
    'They are all on narcotics," he shouted; we laughed
Mario 'Motts' Tonelli—An Italian American Survivor and Servant.................................77
    A college football ring saves a war prisoner's life
Apples Falling from a Big Tree.........................81
    Three generations in a car for ten hours
A Surreal Circle Surrounding Susan....................85
    You decide which is real and which is an illusion
Vini Orlandini, The Tattooed Man, Has Died.............87
    Tattoo signposts from fifty years ago, in quiet surrender
Bedtime Stories for the Grandkids......................93
    At bedtime, grandkids become suddenly dehydrated
Quarantine #6: Numbers on Paper......................97
    Losing the bondage of numbers
My Armenian Aunt Mary...............................99
    'Am I right? Tell me if I am wrong'
Guilty Until Proven Innocent—Sandy the Dog............105
    Birthday cake surprises provided by Sandy the yellow Labrador
Chasing the Sunset...................................113
    We all have to say goodbye
The Persistence of Memory...........................117
    Your grandparents have deep thoughts too

Intro to Diets..121
    "I Am Just the Way I Look Now!"
Reunion: Looking for Dad.........................129
    Dad's shipmates seventy years later
Quarantine #4 We are made of clay —Easter News........139
    A starship, an android, and faith
Long Short Drive to a Sub Sandwich....................141
    Love abandoned for a sub sandwich
Two Stories from the Moon..........................143
    The moon is a harsh mistress
Selling the Business................................145
    Count your career days; they will end someday
In Someone's Living Room or
  "Sit Crooked, But Talk Straight"....................147
    You can't hurt a relative by what you say
Soccer Number Eight in Armenia.....................151
    An unlikely fourteen-year-old hero heals a country
Treasure—The Island House on Nagawicka Lake..........157
    One-hundred-year-old treasure found within a child
"I Am Right, You Are Wrong".......................163
    Fight-or-flight kicks in when we discover we are wrong
The Ageless Phillip Dugas of New Orleans..............169
    An exchange between value and time: which is true treasure?
Buster and George, a Trilogy........................175
    A tapestry of life held on a golf course park bench
Clouds on Bellano Court............................181
    The clouds hold the answer to no question
Acknowledgements................................184
About the Author.................................185

Also by Chuck Hajinian

Sandy and Garbo

Praise from an Unbiased Expert

"A collection of short stories written with a salty flavor that causes your mind to imagine times current and bygone, but yet not distant, of laughter and heartfelt tears. You will learn things. You will start to recall your own stories. Garbo has written a classic masterpiece that will be talked about for years to come. Now that he is done writing this, maybe he can call his mother once in a while?"

–Garbo's mom, Lucy

Introduction

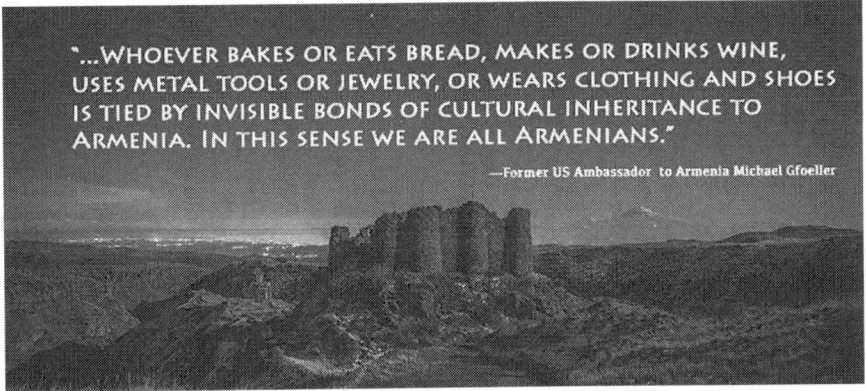

"...WHOEVER BAKES OR EATS BREAD, MAKES OR DRINKS WINE, USES METAL TOOLS OR JEWELRY, OR WEARS CLOTHING AND SHOES IS TIED BY INVISIBLE BONDS OF CULTURAL INHERITANCE TO ARMENIA. IN THIS SENSE WE ARE ALL ARMENIANS."

—Former US Ambassador to Armenia Michael Gfoeller

Before every concert, the orchestra plays notes—out-of-sync notes stretching their fingers or lips on their instruments with their fellow band mates. That is the warmup. Since the pen is mightier than the flute—here is the intro.

Why forty-one short stories? Because who has time for long stories. Most of my relatives have short attention spans. Just kidding. They are just waiting for you to stop talking so they can talk. People like the short emotional punch of short stories. Everyone is busy! This is a buffet of interesting and strange characters, of love lost and love never looked for. Of horrendous conditions overcome with faith and steel determination of ordinary people. This "food" buffet line, you may want to visit twice.

Are these true short stories? All good Armenian stories start with this time-honored saying:

There was a time that was and a time that was not.

Basically, some are completely true, some have true parts, and some are completely made up. You decide.

Storytelling is a lifeline art for all people. It blends the mind, heart, and soul unlike any other medium.

These are my finest stories. They have been accumulating over my lifetime, and they are finally written down and published. You will meet Nazar, my ever-friendly, advice-giving, navy dad. Charlene, my third-grade crush. How about breakfast with Claude Monet? A healing, old dog named Buster. Connie, a lost love when I was young. Vini the Tattooed Man with a funeral twist. How to look skinny—ideas used for centuries. A New Orleans oddity named Phillip Dugas who never ages. And many more. Some were written during The Great Quarantine. These stories are the signposts in my life.

Special thanks to the following, without whose encouragement and laughter, this book would not be in your hands: Patty, Nancy, Gini, Sarah, Kari, Leslie, Ian, Paul, Bill, Lucy, Nazar, Peter, Uncle Hach, Aunt Mary, Dave and Eddi, Levon, Stacy, Auntie Cathy, Merrijo, Lydia, and many more who took the time to be my friend. Finally, my love and partner on this blue-green marble, my soulmate, my reason to wake up each day, my wife, Mary Kay.

To your enjoyment!

Garbo 2-22-2022

Third-Grade Memory Held Captive

Ice skating. Loneliness. Will she like me? Charlene. Ruined painting.

Tap, TAP, Tap …

Wendy sat in the row next to me in my third-grade class at Luther Burbank grade school, a three-story burgundy red brick school built in the 1920s in the middle of our working-class Philadelphia neighborhood. Wendy's beautiful blonde hair fit like a helmet on her eight-year-old head, each hair in perfect alignment, only adding to her angelic beauty. Bright blue eyes, thin pursed lips, and a turned-up nose. Quite observant for an eight-year-old male who had years to go before the tyranny of puberty showed up. All observations were from the neck up. I could smell her perfume even though she was not wearing any. I wanted to marry her, but I realized I did not have a job and was not very good at spelling. I was, however, exceptional in art. At least, that was what I told my teacher because my mom was an artist.

One day, my time arrived. That special moment in the World Series of life when you are called to the plate. The crowd cheers. It is your turn to be the hero.

"Charles, can you come over and help Wendy paint her tiger? She is having trouble mixing colors to make the tiger's skin orange."

Looking up to the whole class, my teacher announces, "Charles's mother is an artist, and he will now help Wendy with her tiger."

Charles. Very formal. Show her how to mix colors to make the tiger skin color. Charles. Named after two uncles on either side of the family. Mom told me to correct anyone who called me Charlie. "The name will stick, and everyone will call you that. Professionally, there are very few Charlies in the real world," she would say as she kept court in her kitchen seven days a week.

Sliding my chair right next to Wendy, she turned her head and smiled. "There is a God," my finite mind rationalized. "Here, Wendy. You mix a bit of purple with yellow, and that will give you the orange color you need. Here let me do it for you."

My eyes never left that turned-up nose of hers and those blue eyes. Colors were mixed and applied to her tiger. The bat swung, and the ball was missed; the crowds left the stadium in a flash as I stared at what I had done. Purple and yellow make brown. Her tiger was now brown. I had ruined her tiger. What happened after that has escaped my memory. I can only guess, a fragile, growing self-esteem shattered? Unanswered, unformed questions were swirling in my eight-year-old brain. I remember Wendy gasping.

After school, Mom in her kitchen asked about my long face. "Nothing, nothing happened; I DON'T want to talk about it!" I declared as I slammed the screen door and climbed into the apple tree right outside the kitchen. That was my oasis. Just me, eight feet up the tree, surrounded by green apples, which I began to eat (eating made problems go away, discovered at the tender age of eight).

When my dad came home, he asked my mom why I was sitting up in the apple tree. After a stressful day managing tough employees, dealing with machines breaking, and a boss giving him all the work, his natural response was often, "Why the hell is he doing that?"

"Something happened at school. He does not want to talk about it."

End of discussion. *Leave it to Beaver* 1950s TV dads were not to be found. My mom would warn my sister and me to stop fighting before my father came home from work. Dad was to be protected, honored, and obeyed.

"Stop fighting because if your dad comes home with all of that work stress and sees you fighting, he will have a heart attack and will die. Is that what you want? You want to give your father a heart attack?" No need for any "time outs." *Your dad could die* ended all the fighting.

My mom would then set the table and fold napkins for the dinner she had been preparing since one in the afternoon.

Soon, winter came to Philadelphia, and Luther Burbank School provided a large, flooded ice-skating rink for the first- to sixth-graders to burn off energy after lunch. I can still see the winter sun reflecting off the snow and shiny ice. I laced up my skates. I was quite a skater. Looking up, there she was with her friends—Wendy! Her blond hair was partially exposed under a pink knitted cap. The ritual would begin. The boys would politely ask the girls if they would like to skate around the rink—one lap, with the option of holding hands! The cool boys in my class and upper classes had no problem approaching a girl, asking, and then turning their heads to show the crowd, "Look who I am skating around the pond with—you could do this too if you had my looks and showered once in a while!"

Should I ask her? my brain questioned. Who do you think you are? She is Wendy. Look at those bangs. Maybe she has forgotten the brown tiger. Are you a Charles or a Charlie? Remember what the teacher wrote on your report card for your parents to see, "Charles is a fine student but NEEDS to show growth in self-control. He visits with his neighbors too much." There it is—no self-control for me. What we have is bigger than both of us, so why fight it?

I skate backward, then do an acrobatic turn around right in front of Wendy and her friends.

Startling them, I look directly with a Clark Gable stare. "Wendy, would you like to skate around the rink with me?"

Did you ever put all the chips on the red square? Did you ever tell the truth and hope there was mercy? This was to be the highlight of my young life up to the third grade. This could determine whether I make it to fourth grade or quit and join the circus.

"No, thanks," and she was gone with her friends. If I could swear, I probably would have said, "Damn tiger—who cares? It's just a painting."

"What's he doing up in the tree again?" my dad asked my mom from our warm kitchen while the winter sun disappeared in the west and lavender shadows colored the tree branches.

"Girl problems," Mom said as she stirred the Armenian Rice Pilaf. Capital letters because we hadn't had a potato in over seven years of my life.

"Girl problems? The kid is eight years old. He needs a job. He has too much time on his hands!" Dad extolled.

"What can a third-grader do?" mom laughed.

"Well, he can start by cleaning his room," Dad distractedly explained.

Cleaning rooms, baseboards, closets, etc. are the recommended therapy for anyone who is depressed, according to the *Armenian Mom and Dad's Almanac for Treating Crushing Sadness*. "Get busy." Once you see how dirty and disorganized your home is, you will realize your problems are minuscule and unimportant compared to a cleaned and organized home. "A place for everything and everything in place."

Not to be outdone, after all, I had a problem in my youth of visiting with my neighbors and not showing self-control. Being pushed by an invisible force, I found myself right in front of another girl in my class. Charlene. Just saying that name—Charlene—is very similar to Charles; maybe that means something. Charlene was just as beautiful as Wendy but in a different way. Wendy was right there. What you see is what you got. Charlene had mysterious eyes shaped like a cat's. She had secrets that even she didn't know about. Her brown hair had an up-flip about three inches above her shoulders that went all around her head. I wondered if she had a marble in that flip. If she tilted her head, would that marble travel around in a semicircle? Now I realize she had a Mona Lisa smile. Was she happy or sad? Was she going to eat the two olives given to us at our hot lunch, or would she give them to me like the ten other classmates? Wait, yes, she put her fingers in the holes where the pits were and placed the olives in the herd of others I had collected. Her smile got bigger.

"What's with the olives?" she sparked as her hand brushed her shiny brown hair to the side of her head.

"Well, I am of Armenian background, and we eat lots of olives because in my grandparents' village, they had an olive press, and that's how they survived ..." Before I could finish my important explanation, everyone had gone to get on their skates and head to the ice rink. I wolfed down ten olives and headed out there.

The bright sun made me shield my eyes as kids were falling and skating, doing figure eights, and laughing. Once my eyes adjusted, I looked up and found Charlene right in front of me. Stop visiting with your neighbor and say something!

"Charlene, would you like to skate around the rink with me?" some uncontrolled voice escaped from deep in my olive-filled gut.

"Sure," she said. Then she did something that opened my heart to the female friendship—she took off her glove and offered me her hand. Fumbling with my oversized leather gloves (my dad was in the leather business, and we were not going to be buying cloth gloves that actually fit a child's hand), I finally freed one hand and oh so gently took her hand in mine.

We skated, she smiled, we skated, her head moving back and forth with each leg going back and forth. Did I mention she smiled at me? I did not want her catching me looking at her, and I had to watch where I was skating—there were other people on the rink. Whether they noticed or not, I would never know. The sun was shining, the winter air was clean, and I was holding a warm hand in mine. We laughed at nothing. Maybe both of us knew something that we didn't. Her mysterious eyes twinkled in the sunlight.

What seemed like forever finally came to an end. The circle lap was complete.

Easing her soft, warm hand out of mine, she tossed a smiling verbal reminder my way. "Thank you, Charles. You are a good skater. Oh, remember red and yellow make orange!" She put on her glove and skated backward, still smiling at me as she slowly disappeared to the snowbanks and our school.

"Thanks, Charlene!" I shouted for the kids unlacing their skates next to me. "Red and yellow make orange. Good skater." My emotions were swirling. Sometimes the brain never catches up with the heart. For that moment, it didn't have to.

Within a few years, I would be torn from my childhood friends and moved as part of the Great Migration to the suburbs, a whole new school in Ardmore just outside of Philadelphia. I would never see these classmates again. Never. Later in life, I would run into someone who followed their careers and ask about them. I was told that Wendy's beauty and popularity continued to mature, and she would become both a Homecoming and Prom queen. Charlene, who lifted me from a nobody to a somebody, would become very popular also.

"Our life journey, no mortal can reveal, results of which, can anyone appeal?"

A car accident in her senior year of high school would claim the life of Charlene. However tragic, she still lives warmly pictured in the etched memory of an eight-year-old who held her hand during one ice-skating lap on a sunny winter day at Luther Burbank grade school.

> *"In the end, today is forever, yesterday is still today, and tomorrow is already today."*
>
> — William Saroyan, *My Heart's in the Highlands*

Pepper on your Caesar

"Would you like some pepper on your Caesar salad?" asks the waiter with the intensity of a surgeon. A large wooden shaker in his hand points toward his white-uniformed shoulder, elbow bent like a spring, ready to crank and sprinkle tiny black rain on my green bowl below.

"No, thank you," I reply as I look up at my date for the evening.

I zero in on her smile framed by her beautiful streaked blond hair. Her lips, covered with white, pink lipstick, are pulled back ever so slightly. The well-lit restaurant seems dim to these old eyes.

"Is it dark in here, or is it just me?" I ask as my fork drives itself into the lettuce.

"Jeff, the sun is shining outside. There are windows—plenty of light," she laughs as she, too, eats her salad and sips her wine.

"I don't know. The older I get, the more light I need to see things," I say. "Don't you remember when you were a kid, and you were always squinting because everything was so bright? It was always sunny when I was a kid," I explain while staring at the large lines around the corners of her eyes. They aren't leaving.

"Who remembers such things from their childhood?" she says. "Your eyes just need more light. It is part of aging."

"Rachael, I need more light in everything now, even my thoughts scatter, and I need light to bring focus ..." My conversation is interrupted by the surgeon waiter.

"Will there be anything else?"

"No, thank you." I look up as he hands me the tab.

Without missing a beat, in my best Groucho Marx imitation while the uniformed waiter with the steel rod back stands right next to me, I look at the check and self-righteously announce, "This is outrageous," and, passing the tab to Rachael, I hammer, "And if I were you, I wouldn't pay it!"

Rachael rolls her gorgeous blue-green eyes.

The Anatomy of a Kiss: Part 1

A fellow comes home and finds his very best friend, BFF, kissing his wife. Eyes bulge, a tear forms. Wringing his hands, he says, "Louie! I have to. But you??!"

When you kiss, your muscles make your cheeks come down slightly and thin them out. Your chin gets longer as the muscles pull your lower lip up slightly. Your upper lip extends down, clearing more space for the nostrils to breathe. Heartbeat increases, puffing up the lips.

Examples of a kiss.

As a seven-year-old with my butch haircut (as bald as you can make a seven-year-old), I ran around the yard until my grandmother, who had just arrived, called me over.

"Hi, Grandma," I said. She hugged me and kissed the top of my head. She held her lips to my head for about five seconds. It seemed like a minute to me. I wanted to go play. She needed to show her affection to the world for her first male grandson. The kiss was not for me. Actually, it was, but I didn't sense what was behind the kiss. I wanted to go play. Was it for her? For her to tell herself that things are okay now?

Forty years earlier, she was reunited with her husband after a separation of seven years due to the Armenian genocide when he found her in the hot, dusty refugee camp. I would imagine they embraced. No story was told about their reunion, and no cell phone or camera picture existed. It would be obvious to all they kissed—a long and hard kiss mingled with tears, great sobs until the tears no longer flowed. Seven years in that kiss. The electricity of skin through clothes, muscles hugging softness and bones—all running up the body's electrical cord, flowing to the edge of the lips. A floodgate of mixed emotions

Between when I got my seven-year-old grandma kiss on the top of my head and my grandparents' embrace-kiss after finding each other, there was another special kiss. This took place in the summer of 1945. It was when her first son, who left as an eighteen-year-old, returned home after fighting for the free world in World War II (so we can have the freedom to hold our opinions along with the obligation to respect the opinions of others). This was the day. The car pulled up. The whole neighborhood was there on the tiny front lawn, surrounded by the simple row houses making up the blocks of South Milwaukee. The hot sun heated the tops of their heads, and the grass was bright green. His father had to work the second shift at the factory and was not allowed to leave—not even for a son coming home from war! Out of the car he emerged with his navy uniform and white navy cap on—two years older and years ahead in maturity. This hardened navy boy-man shook the hands of the neighbors and, like a Hollywood movie, the crowd parted, and there was his mom wearing her large blue navy dress with little white flowers—motionless, ten feet away. He ran to her as his tears dripped to the pavement. They embraced. Her tears again lubricated her kisses on his cheeks. After years of death and war, some in the crowd got letters and visits from the State Department and would never see their sons again. She got her son back. He became my father. Those who were there told me there wasn't a dry eye in the crowd. Strangers, neighbors, relatives, and friends—all sense and experience for themselves when others kiss. Uncontrollable emotions of sadness and joy mingled together—weeping by the neighbors, by his sisters and brother. Kisses do that.

The Anatomy of a Kiss: Part 2

It doesn't matter that the actors who are kissing on the ginormous movie screen are not in love. In fact, they probably hate each other, but the money is good, and they are actors. They are good at pretending. They can lie. Those watching cannot lie. Their heartbeats increase. Their hands get sweaty. Their eyes create a "fight or flight" adrenaline rush. "Do something." Some will squirm, others will fantasize about some kissing event or imagine themselves being kissed by the actor or actress.

Two beautiful, well-made-up people, their lips meet, and the focus becomes those lips. Even the cameraman focuses on those lips. What about her hair or his nicely trimmed hair over his ears? No, the lips, please. We will never match their beauty, but for that moment in time. WE ARE RICHARD BURTON. WE ARE ELIZABETH TAYLOR. Cleopatra and Mark Antony. Who? Never mind. Just Google them. They were the hotties from a time long gone. They are dead now.

There is the European kiss where lips don't touch. Cheeks are the receiving ends of those lips. Both cheeks. One is good; two seals the deal.

Observation: When you kiss, you are vulnerable. You are setting aside your personal wall. You are coming to the peace table. You are surrendering to the opposition. All that you are is on the line. You come down off your hand-built pedestal and realize that even though this body separates you physically, mentally, and emotionally, you still can connect through it all simply by a kiss.

For a period of time, my twelve- to fourteen-year-old nieces and nephews spent some of their summers with us at our lake home. They learned to sail with other teens on the lake, as their parents had done forty years earlier. On one particular beautiful sunny day, the robin's-egg blue sky was dotted by small, puffy mashed-potato clouds that hung like angel observers over the day's events. It was a regatta, and two sailors from Nagawicka Lake had, for the first time in five years, won a race. This required them to come forward, to the applause of over 100 people, and accept a trophy. My fourteen-year-old niece was the crew for the "skipper," a tall fourteen-year-old kid named Mark. Having to spend hours together on the boat, fighting wind, waves, and other boats, they were bonded in battle. The romantic tension was there, apparently observed by many over the sailing summer. Mark and Melissa come forward for the trophy. Mark first, then Melissa behind. Mark and Melissa accept the trophy to the applause and cheers of parents and the other kid sailors. Looking down at his shoes, he looked up to begin his speech of thanks. The crowd was dead silent, eagerly awaiting his words. Before he can say a word, three ten-year-olds in the front row, unable to control their big smiles, shout out for all the 100 people present to hear:

"KISS HER, MARK. YOU KNOW YOU WANT TO!"

We all want to kiss someone—sometimes for them, most times for us—to send a message. We care; we are here to protect. Sometimes it is for selfish self-interest. Our hormones are raging. We are simply aroused and need to burn off that "energy." Food tastes great when you are really, really hungry. Age can diminish taste buds. Try and remember!

Why do people go to horror movies? They want to be scared! They want their blood to pump. They want to feel alive. They want to sweat, scream and squirm in their chair. Usually with friends around. Same thing with kissing, except without friends around. One other person will simply suffice. Kissing is God's way of saying, "Hey, center of the universe, you need someone."

If you can feel good and make someone else feel good, squirm, and emotionally scream, why the hell not?

Consider Judas and Jesus in the Garden of Gethsemane. We are told the Son of God was betrayed by a kiss.

Michael Corleone kissed his brother Frido before he had him killed.

Always give and receive a kiss. Your soul needs the sunshine.

Ladies' Night at Revere's Bar

All small towns are dying. Mom and pop shops have long been eliminated by big box stores. So tonight, in a small town thirty miles outside of Boston proper, "Ladies' Night" has been declared. You see, all the stores are offering wine to lady shoppers tonight. The four-street town is packed with women from two neighboring small towns that begin with a country name and end with a "ville" or "field." It is a good time to be a woman.

Of course, I am alone. I am the only male in the bar. I never got the notice that it was a Night for Ladies—Ladies' Night. Being the odd man out, I strangely feel welcome. I just want a quiet beer in the town's only Irish pub—Revere's. The Irish never settled in this town, nor is it the style of an Irish pub. Lots of light tan oak bar stools and a menu offering non-historical names like "IPA," "Yingling," and odd-sounding names like "Spotted Cow" and "Fat Tire." Genius. Who would name a beer with the word "Fat" or "Cow" in it? Only in Massachusetts, where the women are free to not give a damn about the circumference of a belt that goes around the space between their breasts and their knees.

I can't get a seat as the place is packed with thirty women who are tired of shopping and now want to drink wine sitting down. They have accomplished shopping—looking at things they don't need but feel compelled in their psyche to buy.

"Put it in the bag, here is my charge" gets rid of lots of angst. For that fleeting moment, they are in control of the lesser person who rings up the sale. They are the king, queen in this case, of the cash register and all those who witness the purchase. Suddenly, the hidden irritations of the past few days are gone. The hidden physical flaws that steal their self-esteem have left the room. Or so I imagine. Still, something has been purchased.

"Is this chair taken?" I ask.

"No," replies a dark-haired woman who I would guess was in her early sixties. Her female companion has long blond hair with wavy kinks every inch or so and bumpy skin. Her eyes are too close together. Do wide-apart eyes mean bigger brains? Bars bring out deep questions until the drinks arrive. They have before them two large glasses of white wine. I order an "IPA." Who knows what it will taste like, but for $9.50, it better dance! After a few sips, not bad. I notice all the sports screens, no longer hidden by cigarette smoke from the past. Soup Nazi—"No smoking for you!" All the ladies are talking, some to more than one person at a time.

"He's a horse's ASS!"

"So, I told my boss I need off."

"44 dollars? I've seen it for a lot less."

On one of the TV screens, the Black Hawks are beating the Bruins 3-1 with four minutes left in the third period.

More sips, a gulp, and another IPA.

Senses are losing an awareness of dulling.

Bruins score a goal.

Instead, I begin to notice age. This is not a college bar with young coeds with perky ponytails and the taut calves of long ago.

These are women who have lost estrogen. Well, really, estrogen has left them—like an extremely slow train that left their station. One hardly notices until frames of the movie are compared in slow motion. They are fighting. The skin is collapsing around their mouths. Their once-proud upper lip struggles to maintain a straight line to match the lower lip. That straight line upper lip sums up their future. Eyelids droop. The rosy cheeks are now colored.

Carefree at one time, now the tightrope walking requires much work. Some have gone gray—peace through resignation. Others have dark hair that matches no shades of eyebrows or skin tones. Dark is better than gray. Dark is softer. With soft artistic waves. Gray is a door they don't want to enter, not just yet.

Still others have the sharpie eye makeup that makes the upper lash curl up, giving depth and mystery to the eyes.

A mystery of history.

I am caught staring and quickly turn back to my beer.

The Bruins start a fight. Two hockey players grab each other's jerseys and try and punch each other. They are very fake angry. They are too close. The fists land in the puffed-up jersey. The referees save their insane manhood and break up the fight. Name any other sport you are allowed to punch someone.

More talking, more talking. What could they possibly be discussing so feverishly for so long? Do words soothe the rattled nerves? Are they bonding or brandishing competitive swords?

"Want another one, sir?" asks the waitress. She is fortysomething, tall with no makeup, and is wearing green antlers and a low-cut blouse. Small chest, I guess. Wait, she bends over to wipe down the bar in front of me. Hmm, I was wrong. "Yes, but let me try a Fat Tire." The ad agency has captured another unaware bystander.

There it is! Every Irish bar must have a Guinness mirror. The mirror never lies. An image of a guy whose head is a battle between hair and scalp, and the scalp is winning, with large, wispy purple bags under his eyeglass-covered eyes. His shoulders are hunched over, almost cradling his ears. Loneliness. Weary, the man finishes his Fat Tire. The years have required their pay. If only he could get them back. Sand through the fingers. He gets up and leaves.

Blackhawks win 3-2.

My Great-Grandma Catherine and Teddy Roosevelt

Back row, great-aunt Mariam, daughter Melanie, great-uncle Kevork. Front row, son Hratch, Great-grandmother Catherine. Hratch would be the only survivor of the 1915 Armenian Genocide.

There she is, right in the middle, my great-grandmother Catherine, surrounded by her oldest son, his wife, and her two grandchildren. The phony backdrop is supposed to give the illusion of a grand ancient palace. She lives on a farm on the outskirts of Tomarza, Turkey, a fiercely independent village of a thousand Armenian families. It has been this way for one thousand years when the Byzantine Empire traded eastern buffer Armenian kingdoms for western kingdoms.

She is a Christian but must adapt to the rulers of the empire, and she thus is covered from head to toe in a burka. Only her face, with a noticeably full smile, shows. She shows no teeth. The art of dentures, nor their affordability, have yet to be perfected. Nonetheless, there is a joy that goes beyond straight or missing teeth. Almost as big as her farmed worked large hands is her full heart. We were told that she was widowed at an early age. Perhaps she lost her husband to the great massacres of the Armenians in 1895-96. Nonetheless, she found herself raising four boys and one girl. One of the boys would die before the age of three. My grandfather, the youngest, would have his name changed to that of the recently deceased boy by his mother, Catherine.

Five thousand miles away, unbeknownst to my great-grandmother Catherine, the former president of the United States was preparing for a future whirlwind of disaster in the calm summer of 1915.

President Theodore Roosevelt was visiting military training camps and speaking to young trainees about the need for America to support the Allies in World War I. At that time, America took a neutral military stance. His speeches would be included at the Panama-Pacific International Exposition—a major event of the early twentieth century. He also spoke at War Department instruction camps. Three of his sons would attend Colonel Leonard Wood's civilian military training camp. His speeches were considered radical and unpatriotic by the existing administration. But still Mr. Roosevelt spoke out. Had America acted sooner, the following might not have even taken place.

The above picture was taken in 1915, about three months before the next story takes place.

"What are you doing?" asked my grandmother, walking on a dirt road leading out of their village in what once was Cilician Armenia, now Turkey.

"Knitting my burial clothes," whispered my great-grandmother Catherine, sweating from the wave after wave of sun heat.

"No, we are going to be fine. You, and your two grandchildren with us, we will make it to wherever we are being led," my grandmother coughed out courageously as the white dust kicked up by thousands from her village filled her lungs.

"Tamom, my dear daughter-in-law. I am going to die on this road, but ..." Pausing like the prophets of old, she raised her hands and, reaching up, she placed them on the head of my grandmother, making the sign of the cross and said, "I give you, I lay upon you, the Hajinian family blessings. From generations passed down, I give that to you right now. Go to America and find my son Sarkis. Be blessed. 'Hasnutiun ('Fruition'). May God grant Hasnutiun."

Under those large weather and age-worn hands passed an invisible blessing. A blessing that neither thief, nor animal-like politician, nor hatred-filled soldier could stop. A blessing that continued through the wonderous times of plenty, through laughter, births of babies, and through dancing with pinkies interlaced. Through harvests that were overflowing with grain and wine to times of invasion, separation, rape, and death. Where all you worked for was simply burned and destroyed. Where the very thing on earth that you treasured was simply taken away, and you were left alone. The blessing remained. Intertwined with a deep faith in the God who made the Armenians, whose Armenian mountain—Ararat—He brought His salvation ship, Noah's Ark, to rest. And of all the nations of the world, He would choose the Armenian nation to become the first Christian Nation. A price they paid for each generation thereafter with their blood and that of their loved ones—for 2,000 years. That honor, that heavenly blessing passed through my great-grandmother's hands on that bright sun-beaten, God-forsaken, dry, hot summer day in 1915.

Ever smiling in the only picture we have of my tiny great-grandmother Catherine, she would die shortly after her heartfelt, whispered speech. My grandmother would take her embroidered clothes, her last human expression, her final statement in a handwoven creation. In the midst of mindless slaughter, a work of art would cover her. Her humanity and creativeness rose and conquered. Joining her shortly of starvation and illness would be her granddaughter, four-year-old Melina. The seven-year-old boy Hratch, and, of course, my grandmother would survive.

Four months after the passing of my great-grandmother, Theodore Roosevelt penned these words about the need for America to stop the carnage. These two, they never met; they never knew each other, but they were bound together as a witness to all that is good in the world. His and other people's speeches, like Ambassador to the Ottoman Empire Henry Morgenthau's, would open America's sleepy, self-centered eyes. And when they awoke, evil trembled.

The American people joined the war effort in 1917, and by the early '20s, they and the American government would provide, in today's dollars, over $2.5 billion for relief and help for the Armenians, Assyrians, Greeks, and other survivors. Two of those helped were both of my grandmothers.

> *"The crowning outrage has been committed by the Turks on the Armenians. They have suffered atrocities so hideous that it is difficult to name them, atrocities such as those inflicted upon conquered nations by the followers of Attila and of Genghis Khan. It is dreadful to think that these things can be done and that this nation nevertheless remains 'neutral not only in deed but in thought,' between right and the most hideous wrong, neutral between despairing and hunted people, people whose little children are murdered and their women raped, and the victorious and evil wrongdoers."*
>
> Theodore Roosevelt, November 24, 1915,
> *Fear God and Take Your Part*, pg. 381

Do not let your hearts be troubled. Trust in God; Trust also in me. In my Father's house are many rooms; if it were not so I would not have told you. I am going there to prepare a place for you, I will come back and take you to be with me that you also may be where I am."

Jesus of Nazareth, *Gospel of John, 14:1-2*

Quarantine #1 Observation

Sometime in the 1860s, a group of French impressionist painters gathered before a respected teacher and waited for their first painting lesson. The instructor looked out at the fidgeting group of anxious fellows like football players ready to leave the locker room for the big game. You could slice their excitement. But the old teacher told them to put their paints away. Placing a recently caught fish on a plate before them, he simply uttered, "Study this. Stare and view. Understand this fish—for the next two hours—then you can pick up your brush!"

I sit quarantined. The last time I was quarantined was when I was a year or two old. Polio was the silent, unseen enemy that robbed people of their strength and, in some cases, worse than death, paralyzed them for life. When I was five, I met one of polio's victims on my playground in the city street I grew up. Nine-year-old Jimmy. Jimmy the Cripple, we called him—not to be mean, but to distinguish him from the other Jimmys on the block. Jimmy would stand with his crutches just off the sidewalk, and when someone would ride by on their bike, he would shove his crutch into the spokes or punch at the wheel, resulting in a wobbly crash. My five-year-old mind could not understand his meanness, but now in this quarantine, I do.

The sun is reflecting off the lake—like the French impressionists. I am antsy to do something, but my legs are tired. I have ripped out twenty-five-year-old bushes and moved four yards of stone and dirt. I must sit still. I am forced to stare at the fish. Always right before me, I relook at the water. After four days of gray, cold skies, the sun has appeared. The sky reflected in blue-gray water and, like flashbulbs, the sun's pinpoint rays mark the waves. My mind searches for some kind of order to the dancing sparkles. There isn't one. Still, it is a ballet, a symphony heard by the soul.

    A pause in the pause. For that special moment.

"A First Love"

What does the title say about an understanding of first love? Do we mentally feel that we have advanced and now we are in control of our emotions to evaluate them? First love? True second love? No, really, this is it—third love? Like laughter, some are a giggle, some a ha-ha, some we wet our pants laughing so hard. Is love like that?

"Mrs. Johnson, how do you like your new upper denture?" I asked as I held up the mirror to the ninety-three-year-old nursing home resident.

"Oh, Dr. Bagdassarian, they look wonderful—makes me look younger than I am, don't you think?" she declared while moving her head in different directions to see her new teeth.

"For an eighty-two-year-old, you look pretty good, Mrs. Johnson," I matter-of-factly blurted.

"I am ninety-three years old!" she shouted with a schoolmarm correction.

Not missing a beat, I repeated an oft-used phrase, "Come on. Why do you ladies insist on making up older ages? You can't fool me; I have your medical chart!"

We laughed, and both of us felt good inside.

"I know you are widowed but watch out with that smile. Lots of suitors will be coming around."

"You know, doctor, there are so few men around the home, the pickings are few. There are two out of the eighty people in the home, and they would be quite popular, but they aren't in good shape," she explained.

Upon leaving the nursing home, my thoughts were interrupted by a distant sight—a memory of recognition, a visual blip that startles the brain and erases the river of existing thoughts.

There she was, getting closer and closer. Could this be Connie?

Our eyes met across a bridge spanning fifty years of time.

I stopped and whispered, "Connie?"

She stopped, "Charlie Bagdassarian?"

The nanosecond where the mind flashes back between breaths and conversations. The electric subconscious feeds the thoughts.

Long before my tour of Vietnam, dental school, my wife Mary Anne, there was this amazing late-1960s activist, songwriter, and protest movement leader. I met this girl with the long auburn hair at the University of Santa Barbara. She caught my eye with her guitar and singing in the café bars of the campus strip and marching with any group that was downtrodden. Her goal was to raise the consciousness of the student body or anyone else who would listen to her about the need to see outside of ourselves.

She sang like Joni Mitchell but had much fuller hips and a large, soft bosom to match. Her voice captured my heart, brain, and body like the sea nymphs of ancient Greece. She was more than my girlfriend; she was my comfort when the uncertainty of a future battled my psyche. When my mother died after a long battle with some form of unknown cancer, her angel arms were around me, her chest was my pillow. Her voice sang poetry that made the world go away.

"Connie, what are you doing at the nursing home? I am so surprised to see you!" I was unable to contain my enthusiasm.

"Oh Charlie, I can't believe it is you after what, forty-five years?" She reached out and hugged me with both arms.

I held her. She held me. We didn't let go. Emotional arousal brought out more than our romantic memories. The lyrics from the Harry Chapin song "Taxi" came to mind:

"We learned about love in the back of a Dodge, the lessons never went too far."

We had romance. This was the late '60s. Although I never had a Dodge. Our bond was deeper. Sure, there were make-out sessions.

Hormones raged. But we had deep discussions from the core of our souls: The war in Vietnam, the new role of women in a man's world, oppression. Jesus Christ, the unjust society. We talked and talked, drank wine and coffee, and talked.

As I snapped back to the present, our embrace finally ended. We both smoothed our clothes.

"Charlie, my husband, is cared for at this nursing home. He developed Alzheimer's when he was fifty-seven. That was eight years ago. He doesn't know who I am. I have cared for him for as long as I could. Then I had to bring him here—Santa Barbara Senior Care Center," speaking like a TV commercial ad woman.

"Well, at least you have the ocean view you always loved at college," I mentioned as I tried to lift her spirits. Will it work?

"Yes, water, water makes everything clean. We set out to change the world, Charlie. You left for Vietnam, and I married this musician who became the love of my life. Now, he hasn't been able to feed himself for two years. Change comes along beyond our well-thought-out plans. Change comes hard. What about you, my Charlie Bear?"

"Charlie Bear? I haven't had anyone call me that in a hundred years. 'Punky,' that's what I called you. We had something amazing, Punky. The whole world waited for our beautiful solutions. After we solved those problems, we looked for that perfect feeling in each other's eyes."

"Yes, and you used that to make our lips meet."

"Me? You were the vixen who charmed me with that beautiful voice."

"What happened to you, Charlie? We broke up over your choice to go to Vietnam. You went there. I continued with the protest songs. What happened to you?"

"Connie, sometimes a voice inside says this is the right thing to do. This is a righteous act. Others don't agree. It was more than a calling. I can't explain even now. Someone in my platoon stepped on a mine and bought the farm. I was wounded quite badly and sent back to San Diego all bandaged up. I married my nurse, Mary Anne, and went to dental school. We have three daughters who live near us in

Mission Canyon and Isla Vista. I still practice dentistry and help out at the nursing home. I want you to meet her, Connie. Over the years, I have told her about you. Here is our number. Please call us."

"Charlie, I would love that. My husband can provide nothing for me. Charlie, we don't, can't communicate in the ways we used to. My vigorous, high-energy life is trapped in his lost mind. People ask me all the time why I stay with him."

"What do you tell them?"

She paused, looked up, then down, then those amazing blue-green eyes locked on mine. "I love him. I simply love him"

A tear formed in my left eye, which I quickly wiped away. That's the Connie I have always loved, always thought of when the shrapnel cut through my leg and back, and sometimes thought of when the sun was setting over the ocean, and a certain peace welled up inside.

Taking both of her hands, we embraced once more. Cheek to cheek, tear to tear.

"Call us, Punky."

"I will, Charlie Bear."

She turned and disappeared into the Santa Barbara Senior Care Center. I got into my Dodge and drove away.

The Night Before the Battle of Avarayr

Who today would die for what they believe? If every opinion is valid, what gain is there for dying for a thought, an idea? Well, these are questions faced by men and women for centuries. Here is one of the first lines drawn in the sand for faith.

One of the most famous and first battles for the right to worship as a man sees fit was fought on Armenian soil on May 26, 451AD. This took place on the Avarayr Plain in the region of the Artaz region of Armenia. Led by Commander Vartan Mamikonian with 66,000 Armenians, made up of 10,000 infantry soldiers, common men, clergy, women, and even the daughters of princes who owned the lands. Together they defended the homeland against the overwhelming odds of over 330,000 Persian troops who also had herds of elephants that were used as crushing weapons.

The Persians were led by King Yazdegerd II, who was married to his own daughter and whom he eventually put to death. This fanatical leader wanted to destroy Christianity and Jewry and have the Armenians worship fire as they did. Idolatry brings with it perversions. Armenians would submit to their cruel rule; they would pay taxes but would not give up the Jesus who redeemed them. Their devotion to Christ, known throughout the ancient world, caused tremendous anger and wrath within the polluted mind and heart of King Yazdegerd II. Unrecorded, perhaps these conversations took place amongst the young Armenian soldiers and their captain the night before the most famous battle in Armenian and Christian world history:

Captain Khoren: Vahan, Nerses, where are you?

Nerses and Vahan: (Quietly) We are here over here.

Captain Khoren: Where?

Nerses and Vahan: To your left. Grab his arm; we are to your left.

Captain Khoren: The Persians across the river have fires lighting the night air, dedicated to their twin gods. We have complete darkness. This darkness is ridiculous. I have been looking all over for you. Did you hear the news? Tomorrow, we fight!

Vahan: No, no, NO! You can't be serious

Captain Khoren: Yes, yes, I heard it from the lips of Sardabed Commander Vartan himself.

Vahan: NO! What about all the negotiations? I thought the Nakharars, the princes who own the land, would work out a solution. Their own daughters are amongst us, ready to fight. Don't they care about their daughters? And these Persians! We have been paying our taxes to them. We honor and bow before their leaders and cult priests on streets that belong to us.

Nerses: (Sighs) I thought having all of us camp out, that this was just a show of strength, to make the Persians bargain. You know, we are serious about our faith.

Captain Khoren: Sharpen your sword on the necks of the enemy. The Persians come tomorrow.

Nerses: (Waving his arms) No, no, no!

Captain Khoren: What is the matter, my brave Nerses?

Nerses: Why now? Can't they talk for another few months? My fields and trees are ready to be harvested. We will be financially ruined! We have markets that are waiting for the fresh fruit.

Captain Khoren: Fresh fruit? What are you talking about? Our faith is at stake here. What is wrong with you two?

Nerses: Faith? You see their campfires? Do you see their elephants outlined in the dark by those fires? Captain Khoren, they have elephants! How will we fight against those beasts that crush the heads of their enemy when they charge? They are worshiping those fires they have created! They are yelling and getting all worked up! How do we fight against such crazed animal men?

Vahan: Khoren, you know the reports, the Persians outnumber us 10-1. I have a two-year-old son at home, and Nerses has five children under the age of ten!

Nerses: When our blood is spilled, who will care for them? While in the presence of the Persian king and nobles, even Sardabed Vartan accepted the fire-worshiping religion to protect his family. Then, when he got back to Armenia, he and the princes let it be known they will always be Christian. Why can't there be a compromise?

Captain Khoren: Did Jesus, the king of all, look for a compromise when He went to the cross for you and your families? For your parents, for your grandparents? If God Himself would suffer beatings and forty lashes from a whip covered with rough dog bones and have metal spikes driven through His wrists and ankles, for what? For miserable jars of clay like you and me? What can we give in return that would equal such a sacrifice? Nothing. Not even our worthless lives would match such a gift.

Vahan: (Stands in front of Khoren) Lower your voice, Captain Khoren. Get this straight: I am not afraid to die. But what will the Persians do to my wife and family after I lie dead on the fields of Avarayr? (Vahan breaks down and sobs).

Captain Khoren: Vahan, let not your heart be troubled. I, too, have a family. Nerses, I, too, am leaving a prosperous business that was handed down for five generations. Besides, who says we will die? Look at these muscles and this sword!

Nerses: Word is spreading fast as to how the Persians treat their prisoners.

Vahan: Yes, they place them in a sack with a snake, a dog, and a cat.

Nerses: Then they drop the sack into a deep river. Right in front of us is the river Tl'mout.

Captain Khoren: Enough of that Vasag talk! I will not let that happen to either of you. Every generation of Armenians is called to fight for some cause or king's whim. Usually an earthly king, over some ridiculous valley or mountain. I have seen those battles. I have fought in them. We suffer and bleed for what? These rocks or that pile of dirt. Listen to me and listen well. This time it is different. This time we fight for our eternity. This time we fight for the God who made us, who put the stars in place and the snow on the caps of Mount Ararat. He brought us His Apostles—St. Thaddeus and St. Bartholomew. Why did he choose the Armenians? Why not the thousand other people of that time? If we have to, what better way to leave this place than defending the name of the Holy Trinity against the evil fire-worshiping Persians and all their perversions? It is better to die for righteousness's sake. We will leave the mortal for the immortal. To live forever.

Nerses: When this is all done, all our families will have this faith! It is hard for me to imagine. I have a pit in my stomach; my head is spinning.

Vahan: The Ghevontian priests tell us that all that we see should help us to trust our God for all that we do not see. They are with us on the very front lines. We fight for the real and unseen.

Captain Khoren: Right you are, my little Vahan. Small in stature but a Hercules giant in faith. Come here, Nerses. Take this yogurt. It will calm your stomach. Breathe deep, relax your mind. This battle is not yours. It is for your families, your animals, your neighbors that you fight. We will win this battle.

Vahan: Some have whispered that God had planned this battle fifty years ago when He provided the Bible to be translated into Armenian for all to read. Since that time, our faith as a nation has grown beyond measure. My grandmother used to read to me from that book.

Nerses: Your grandmother was preparing you for this. Perhaps now is the time for that faith to be tested. You can show her that you understood. She, along with the angels, they are watching over us.

Captain Khoren: I, too, am a man just like you two. I, too, have fears and doubts. If I could be anywhere else, under different circumstances, surely, I would leave. But Saradabed Vartan told his captains to tell all of you that our Christianity, our love of the Holy Trinity, is like our skin and cannot be separated. God is with us. Many miracles have taken place these last few months. He has prepared us for this moment. The Holy Spirit hovers over all of us, ready to fill us with the strength to face what God has in store for those who love Him. For some, Christ is just a name, but for us, He is not only our Lord but our Brother. We are not fighting for a concept or a good feeling. The object of our faith is alive. He hears this conversation as we speak. He will be with us. He will go before us. He will take care of our families in ways we cannot. Better is one day in the courts of His kingdom than a lifetime walking on this dry land. Again, I know we will win this battle.

Vahan: Come, Nerses. Let us prepare for tomorrow. Captain Khoren is right. Perhaps we can win this battle. Our courage will make our families' faith stronger and be a testimony to those who chose to walk in the light of Christ. Whether we are remembered or not, this is our moment in history.

Nerses: Thank you, Captain Khoren; this I know. I have never felt more alive than at this very moment. Tomorrow we will see.

The famous Battle of Avarayr lasted only one day and has been listed as a horrendously vicious and bloody battle. Each army fought with uncontrolled rage and animal ferocity. Elephants and 330,000 Persians descended upon the hapless Armenian infantry of 10,000. The screams and shouts, the dust and wind, contributed to the surreal battle scene. The Armenians inflicted huge losses on the Persians to the point that even though the Armenians lost the battle, the Persians eventually stopped their efforts to convert Armenians to Zoroastrianism. Over 1,036 Armenian soldiers fell that day, including Commander Vartan. For the next thirty years, Vartan's nephew Vahan would struggle in hit-and-run warfare against the Persian occupiers until the Treaty of Nvarsag, which granted the Armenian nation religious freedom and home rule. This proceeded the Magna Carta by 750 years. Each year, the 1,036 martyrs are recognized by the Armenian Orthodox churches. Though unnamed, a Nerses, a Vahan, and a captain named Khoren most likely took their place amongst those who received the title "Good and Faithful servant," while an ethereal crown was placed on their heads that day.

Garbo Sit-Down Comedy

The jokes are original, but the people who originated them died long ago. I know these jokes work. I have heard other comedians use them. No joke is original. Romans had comedy clubs, but if you bombed, you ended up being given a sword and a shield, and you got to fight a gladiator. I reuse other people's jokes. Just like the symphonies keep playing Beethoven's Fifth and multiple restaurants serve this thing called "a hamburger." No one gets upset about that. McDonald's never calls Burger King and says, "knock it off!"

So here are some things I find funny:

Haig Asadourian was coming into America through Ellis Island. All immigrants were given an eye test with an eye chart. The doctor showed Haig the eye chart and asked him to read the letters.

Haig started, "K-I-R-O-U-D-J-A-K-M-A-D-J-I-A-N." The doctor said, "You know those letters pretty well." Haig said, "Know them? I dated his daughter!"

A recent study has found women who carry a little extra weight live longer than men who mention it.

My mother was eighty-eight years old. She never used glasses. Drank right out of the bottle.

A very old man goes to the urologist and says, "I can't pee." The urologist asks him how old he is. The man replies, "Ninety-three." The urologist says, "You have peed enough!"

An old Armenian woman who was a seamstress is walking home, and a flasher walks right up to her, opens his coat, and exposes himself. She shouts, "You call that a lining?!"

Sayings of the Armenian Buddhist:

If there is no self, whose arthritis is this?

Be here now. Be someplace else later. Is that so complicated?

Wherever you go, there you are. Your luggage is another story.

The convict was about to go to the electric chair. He called his lawyer for advice. The lawyer says, "Don't sit down."

I remember in psychology class reading about Pavlov's dogs. I thought how stupid those dogs were. Then the bell rang, and we went to lunch

You think it's bad now? In twenty years, our country will be run by people home-schooled by day drinkers.

Why don't you ever see the headline "Psychic Wins Lottery"?

My wife is so suspicious, she looked at my calendar and wanted to know who May was.

To save our marriage, we went to a workshop. I went to work, she went to shop.

Old country Armenian husband to wife, "Stick to your washing, ironing, cooking, and scrubbing. No wife of mine is going to work."

People call me a hypochondriac, which really hurts.

My wife's on a banana and coconut diet. She hasn't lost weight, but boy, can she climb trees!

I was sitting next to a big Armenian woman with the largest diamond necklace I had ever seen. "Excuse me," I said, "but that is one big, beautiful diamond. It looks like the Hope Diamond!" She replied, "This is the Antramian Diamond, and like the Hope Diamond, it comes with a curse!" I asked what the curse was. She told me, "Mr. Antramaian!"

Never moon a werewolf.

If at first you don't succeed, skydiving is not for you!

Progress is made by lazy men looking for an easier way to do things.

My psychiatrist says I have a revenge problem. Well, we will see about that.

This morning I saw a neighbor talking to her cat. It was obvious she thought her cat understood her. I came into my house and told my dog. We laughed a lot.

Tall Short Stories from the Comedic Mind of Garbo

Did you know?

By replacing your potato chips with grapefruit as a snack you can lose up to 90% of what little joy you still have left in your life.

DOES THE JELLY IN A DONUT COUNT AS A SERVING OF FRUIT?

ASKING FOR A FRIEND.

INTERESTED IN TIME TRAVEL?

Meet Here Last Thursday, 7pm

Tea for Two on the Putting Green of Life

"The greatest happiness you can have is knowing that you do not necessarily require happiness."

William Saroyan, My Heart's in the Highlands

The fall sunlight cast a soft, deep green shadow. The shadow was created by an eightysomething, white-haired lady in long pink shorts and a blue sweater vest with a patterned golf shirt, collar turned up. She was putting. Her head down, she didn't notice me on the expansive carpet of yellow-green manicured grass.

I dropped my golf balls and wanted to begin my putting routine when conflicting thoughts popped into my head. Thoughts are good. Very good. It means you still are connected above the ground. I was here to relax and feel good about my putting ability—think only about pushing a white ball over a grassy green surface into a cup. That was the only goal.

However, over-eager electrical pulses erupted in the ocean called my brain. Each pulse-thought had a point to make.

"Hey, mister hot shot golfer: did you say hi to that lady?"

"I'm just here to putt and get into my own thoughts—you know: How did I sleep? What are my plans for tonight? How are the grandkids? I think something hurts on my body …"

"Hey, center of the earth buddy: what about that lady? Maybe she is a recent widow. Could she be thinking about her lost husband? Or maybe she has major health problems?"

"So what? What is that to me? If I want to play well and feel good about myself, I have to get that white ball to obey my thoughts and sink into that hole."

"Just perhaps that lady lives alone and has not had human, face-to-face contact in a few days. Maybe her family has forgotten her. Maybe she could use a smile, a compliment, a human touch?"

The last electric, nonrecordable thought won the battle. It makes sense: golfers have a special bond. We are soldiers in a war to get a white ball into a four-inch hole, fighting through trees, sand bunkers, and unseen curves in the greens. Sometimes we get caught in the rain; sometimes we get sand in our eyes. The sun can be tough too. Courage comes to mind—the courage to reach out to a fellow golf course soldier in need. Feeling like a regular Bob Hope, Bob Costas, Johnny Carson, or some other master of ceremonies of today or yesteryear, I walk over and stop about fifteen feet away. With hands on my hips, I let out a soft greeting that fits well with the warm, fall breeze which suddenly arose.

"Beautiful fall day for golf. We won't have too many days like these in New Hampshire!"

She stopped putting, bent her knees, and picked up her ball. Turned very slowly and walked away.

A Hero for All of Us—
Shavarsh Karapetyan

A trolley bus collapses into a lagoon in 1976. Shavarsh Karpetyan, champion swimmer.

Mary Kay Hajinian and Shavarsh Karapetyan at SOAR Special Olympics.

The trolly bus's back window was smashed open by the strong kick of this twenty-three-year-old Soviet Armenia National Finswimming Champion. Blood began to pour out of his torn flesh.

"The shoe order is ready for the Chobanian family," shouts Shavarsh. His youthful figure has long been replaced by a rotund, broad-shouldered man in his fifties. His chest and belly reach the counter first. His eyes still sparkle. The Chobanian lady picks up her shoe order. He lives in and owns a shoe factory in Moscow. Few recognize this hero of the old Soviet Union. This is a hero of Armenia.

Armenians always talk about their heroes. Most have long passed. This way, the hero is protected, not to be hurt when the usual Armenian debate emerges. "What hero? He didn't care for his own mother. What did he do for the city? He didn't fight in a war! Sarkis did. He is a real hero!"

Of the eight million Armenians scattered over the world, few would be able to tell Shavarsh's story today. The internet is a wonderful thing. By chance, while viewing an Armenian culture page, I came across his amazing story.

No one else dominated the Armenian sports scene from 1972-76 like Shavarsh. During that time, he broke several world records and won eight gold medals at the European Finswimming Championships. This is a sport in which swimmers move through the water with a whale-shaped fin over their feet. Shavarsh had an amazing ability to hold his breath and propel himself.

In 1976, after running eight vigorous miles with his brother, the two noticed that a trolley bus had left the road over a bridge and tumbled into a lagoon pond. Only the poles of the bus were visible.

Without a second thought, Shavarsh jumped in and found the trolly with sixty-seven passengers filling up with water quickly. His strong legs and feet pounded against the glass of the back end of the trolley—one kick, two kicks, finally, the third powerful kick broke the glass, and he quickly swam into the darkness of the dirty water and grabbed a passenger. Leading them to the surface, he took five deep breaths. Back down again through the jagged frame that once held a window. This was the gate of hell or the gate of heaven. Grabbing another, this one a child, he would again make his way to the surface, where his brother would help revive and bring to life these poor souls.

This procession from hell to heaven continued for twenty-one people until Shavarsh could swim no more. With blood oozing from his flesh, torn by the jagged glass, he collapsed. Authorities would arrive. Ambulances and hospital personnel would save these rescued people—twenty-one in all. Another forty-six would perish in this water lagoon grave. Shavarsh himself would spike a high fever. He was hospitalized and unable to walk for over three weeks. Those weeks were spent fighting for his own life due to the infections from the dirty pond water.

During Soviet times, tragedies did not make front-page news. Anything that would shed a bad light on the government would be avoided. Why would the trolley collapse into the lagoon? What went wrong? Who was responsible? Hiding this incident also meant hiding the heroic actions of Shavarsh. He never looked for acknowledgment; he would pay an undeserving price for his actions.

With hard training, he would come back and win, but he could no longer swim as he did in the past. In 1977, he would compete in the European Championships and other events and win three silver medals and one gold medal. Still, he was not the same. His torn-up legs and the damage to his lungs ended this young man's dreams and career.

Who knows how far he could have gone in the Olympics against a world champion like Mark Spitz? We will never know. Eventually, the truth cannot be contained. Word spread among the Armenians. A hero, a nonwar hero, was in their midst.

Soon the outcry became too strong for the central government to deny. Shavarsh would get his medals. He would become a hero of the Soviet Union.

This common man was walking when he noticed a burning house. Not hesitating, he would rush in and save four people. He would then continue to search for more. The ambulances took the family to the hospital. They would also take Shavarsh, who would come away with second- and third-degree burns on his arms and body.

His countrymen never forgot him, and in 2014, he was honored by giving him the right to carry the Olympic Torch into the Kremlin ahead of the Winter Games in Sochi. He proudly said he was carrying the torch for both Russia and Armenia.

In 2018, I asked if the finest worldwide organization that raises money for Armenian orphans—SOAR, the Society for Orphaned Armenian Relief—if they would sponsor a Special Olympics for handicapped orphans. They agreed and called their recurring event "I Can." I then asked if they could locate Shavarsh Karapetyan. They were surprised that I would know about him. The call was sent to him in Moscow. Would he be the master of ceremonies and the main newspaper draw for ignored handicapped orphans?

"Of course," he replied.

We would eventually meet, and he would ask me through an interpreter why I chose him for the event. He had his faults; he would try and explain. I told him that these kids needed a hero. We were all flawed when our lives are examined under a magnifying glass. I told him that he would be rescuing these kids from loneliness, from sadness and the grief of handling their handicaps, without a mom or dad present.

For three days, Shavarsh would hug the ladies, shake hands with the men, and embrace the 120 handicapped orphan children of Armenia who had been shuttered in institutions by their countrymen and, in some cases, their families. They were living six to eight in a room in large institutional settings of a leftover Soviet orphanage system. Some were in wheelchairs. Thoughts were permanently scrambled for some. Others could not fully communicate. Then there were those who would never leave a wheelchair. All were groomed with hair combed and smiles on their cleaned faces. They would play their hearts out in dragon boat races, soccer matches, basketball, and many other Olympic events. Those who cared for them were true angels. Their love and commitment to these children shown like the bright sun that bathed the outside events.

The time for Shavarsh to address the children and all of us had arrived. His speech to them was in Armenian, which I do not speak. Essentially, I was told this was his message: "Those who have participated, they are the winners. They showed they can, together with all of you, I also can. We all can be happy. We must do our best, and most important is to love—love to our motherland, to our parents, and love in general. You can do everything you can imagine. Let nothing hold you back."

Looking at the children, tears were in our eyes. This man also cried. Sometimes our heroes do not always carry weapons. Sometimes they do not demand world attention. Some just do what is right at the time they are called. That is Shavarsh, my true Armenian hero.

Breakfast with Claude Monet 1922

It was 1922, and I was staying with Claude Monet at his studio at Giverny. We had just eaten breakfast when I told him that Degas, who died five years earlier, refused to be a slave to nature. Claude turned to me and said, "Degas, on his death bed, wanted to know who the jackass was who purchased one of his paintings for 10,000 francs." I told Claude there are no straight lines in nature and that he should try to use Hansa Light Yellow to capture the sunshine. He laughed, and this photo was captured as we left the table and walked into his studio. Within four years, he would pass away. I am the only one left.

Quarantine Short Story #9

Listening to Distant Tambourines

Hajinians have always had a strong and certain zest for living. In Armenian, we say *kef ghee*—a person who is always for a party—not in a drunken orgy of indulgence like other unnamed ethnic groups. There is too much fun to be retold at future parties to lose in a black hole of lost memory. Armenians will have a drink, but only for lubrication and not suffocation. When my father was in college at San Jose State in California, he had very little money or food. His old college roommate shared the story of how they would crash Armenian weddings to get a good meal, drink, and dance. With lots of pretty and not-so-pretty Armenian girls on display at these weddings, the adults welcomed the party crashers as possible suitors for their daughters.

My father had a great uncle-cousin—a distant relative on his mother's side—whom he was named after: Nazar Salbashian. He was called *Nazar Di-ee—Di-ee,* meaning uncle in Turkish. He was known as a *Kef Ghee*. A *Kef Ghee* is the type of person you want to hang around with—always fun, always looking for a fun party, a people lover. There is a rare *Kef Ghee* gene. Most people are unaware of it, and most do not have it. He had it. In the old country, he rode an impressive white horse around the village as a sign of importance and notice. The problem was *Nazar DI-ee* had no money-making skills, no formal education, or notable talents except to create a joyful moment anywhere he went. When I was six years old, we went to California to experience and visit Uncle *Nazar Di-ee*. He was about ninety years old. He had the most sparkling, penetrating blue eyes. When he saw us get out of our car, tears ran down his face as he raised his bent arms over his bald and sun-dried head and began to snap his fingers and dance. He was a great Armenian "pinky in the air" dancer. Most times, he had a tambourine by his side with his other finger-snapping hand raised in the air.

Once the dancing and finger snapping stopped, having not seen each other for over ten years, the two Nazars embraced and wept.

He and his wife, Goulizar, were unable to have children. My father was the closest thing to him as the son they never had. When they lived in South Milwaukee, Wisconsin, in the late '20s and early '30s, my eight-year-old father would help him deliver ice for the iceboxes to families. My dad's job was to guard the truck while *Nazar Di-ee* delivered the ice. On some occasions, if the women were particularly attractive, the visits took a little longer. The gift of gab. Later, he would buy my dad an ice cream for his silence.

Moving to California, *Nazar Di-ee* was surrounded by thousands of Armenians, many of whom were multimillionaires in the 1950s due to buying prime California farmland in the 1920s. Now, in the fall and winter of their lives, these men wanted to enjoy the fruits of their labor. *Nazar-Di-ee* was their man. The party took place in the hot, dusty packing houses of 1950s Fresno, California. He had no money for their poker games. They would give him money to play. He would lose that money and tell his friends he had to go because he had no money. "Sit down, here's some *tram* (Armenian word for dollar)—keep playing." Which he did. But not before picking up his tambourine and banging it on his leg while singing an Armenian love and drinking song while his other hand waved back and forth. They loved him. When he finally left, he would help himself to a crate of walnuts and pomegranates as his fee for the entertainment. Each year around Thanksgiving, he would send us a box of pomegranates, walnuts, and walnuts/grape fruit rollups. My father would send a gift of $50 to him and his wife in the early '60s.

I cannot sit still. I am a lonely dog. I need people. Who wants to just read a book? I can read a book after the visiting people leave. Or read it when there is a snowstorm, or some plague keeps me isolated.

"Can we have some people over?" I ask my war-torn wife after days, months and years of nonstop entertaining.

"Can't you just sit and read something? People, people, all the time people. Alright, but you have to clean up when they leave," she surrenders.

I raise my hands and snap my fingers. I hear the distant tambourines of uncle *Nazar Di-ee*.

Chapter Eternal for Nazar Hajinian

Nazar Hajinian
At the Lake

"How about you, Nazar? Have you given your life to Jesus Christ?" asked the full-bodied and tall Armenian successful businessman-turned-Pentecostal evangelist Demos Shakarian. Standing next to him at the podium in the medium-sized room in the back of a family restaurant stood my dad, exactly one head shorter. No cathedral with stained glass windows or soaring pillars and marble floors. The carpet was stained with restaurant traffic. Demos had just given a rousing gospel message to a crowd of 150 people. Their attention was captured.

Fifty-five years earlier, this fellow, my dad, was born to Armenian immigrants. Twelve years before his birth, his mother was separated from his father for seven years during the Armenian Genocide. They eventually made it to a place of peace in Wisconsin. My grandparents and their two young daughters lived in a home in the village outside of South Milwaukee called Carrollville. It was a community of tiny homes built for the laborers by the owners of the Peter Cooper Glue works. This is where my grandfather worked—pushing carts filled with horse carcasses from one end of the factory to another—second shift. Under the Ottoman Empire's policy, Christian children were not allowed to get an education. My grandfather could neither read nor write, yet he traveled over three continents and empires to make money and bring his bride to America. Small of stature, he was a brilliant, street-smart man.

Around 1924, grandmother, while living in Carrollville, went into a state of depression after hearing about the loss of her beloved brother. A burst appendix brought a quick death to him. This death sentence was common during times before penicillin. He was studying to be a dentist in Aleppo, Syria. The older Armenian ladies came around and viewed her palpable sadness and inactivity and scolded her. The rule of that day was tough love for a woman who witnessed so much death and destruction in her fragile early years. Bootstraps were reachable.

The conversation most likely went: "You have two young daughters. You are neglecting them. Where is your brother? He is with our Lord. Enough of the sadness!"

The other solution they gave her, which to this day is utilized to rid the extended Hajinian family of grief, feeling sorry for yourself, depression, etc. …

"Keep busy, clean the house, stoop down and clean the baseboards. Clean, clean, clean, and all your sadness will dissipate." You might have a depressing personality, but at least your house was clean in case you cheered up and invited someone over.

Apparently, it worked as my grandmother got pregnant and delivered my father into this world about nine months later, in 1925. She named him Nazar, after her brother, who had rescued her during the Genocide times—times no human should ever experience. Separated from her two younger brothers, not knowing if they were dead or alive, she clung to her brother Nazar who would find and rescue her. Now that he was gone, she gave birth to a new Nazar—a Christian name and short for Nazareth, where Jesus lived and worked. My father spoke no English until he started kindergarten at the age of five. He had no real need to speak English. The neighborhood where he grew up was filled with displaced, tortured, and illiterate Armenians whose only hope was the freedom of America. What did they find in this new country called America? Freedom to worship, freedom from persecution in all of its forms, from restrictions on education to penalty taxes for being Christian. But prosperity would take another generation. Tough foundry jobs working second shifts, menial dirty labor awaited most of them. The Roaring Twenties passed them by—no short-skirt flapper dancing, no rising stock market rewards. The Great Depression, however, ground into them like a stone threshing floor. With 25 percent unemployment, these Armenian men were the first to be let go. No unemployment insurance, no severance packages, nothing. The state would provide jars of peanut butter, wagons of fruit, and clothes. Coal to heat their homes was also provided. Unable to pay their mortgages, they would lose their homes. Some had seventy percent equity built up. It didn't matter. The bank took their houses, and they were forced to move out. They survived by state welfare. President Roosevelt became their hero. And in return, these immigrant Armenians would provide their sons for the battlefields of World War II. These boys, like tens of thousands of other American boys, would die on the distant hills in the Philippines, on the beaches of Normandy, and in the planes that bombed the enemies of our country. I know of Armenian husbands and wives who lost their beloved children in the Genocide, small little innocent children, only to start a new family in America and to again lose their son to a bullet or a bomb in World War II.

Where is the oasis? Where is the balm for the soul? When the flowing tears are no more, and the human spirit is devoured, when the heart wants to quit beating and the mind can take no more, where did these Armenians turn? Some turned to the church, which opened the door to their only hope, the One who understood, who could fill the emptiness that nothing in this world could. They turned to Christ as their fathers and their fathers before them.

Again, Demos asked my dad that question, "How about you, Nazar? Have you given your life to Jesus Christ?"

My father paused and looked down. This was a man who was raised in the Armenian Orthodox Church. His country was the first Christian nation in the whole world. He knew of the 1.5 million Armenian Christians who were slaughtered because they would not change their name from being Christian and embrace the official religion of the Ottoman Empire—Islam. His grandmother, uncles, cousins, and others were listed amongst the Martyrs and now Saints of Heaven. He sat through Divine Liturgies as a child and adult. Two hours of worship in Classical Armenian that few understood. During the Divine Liturgy, he sang in the pew songs reserved for the choir. He went forward for Communion each and every time. As an eighteen-year-old, he carried the Navy Man's Prayer Book in his pocket when he slept. He held that book while on the deck of the destroyer, the *USS The Sullivans,* while kamikaze pilots flew over his head, seeking out great prey like an aircraft carrier to bomb and bring death.

On December 18, 1944, the greatest typhoon to hit the US Navy, Typhoon Cobra, created the worst natural disaster in US Navy history.

It struck the fleet my father was a part of. The admiral of the fleet, not having modern weather technology, ordered the fleet to sail in the direction of the oncoming storm. The full fleet of aircraft carriers, battleships, and five destroyers headed into the 200-mile-an-hour wind. Two destroyers were able to fill up with fuel.

When the storm had passed, three destroyer ships were no longer visible. They had been torn in half or flipped over. Over seven hundred seamen had perished. My father's ship, the *USS The Sullivans*, named after the five Sullivan brothers who all perished on the ship the *Juneau* in 1942, had miraculously survived. It had been filled up with fuel and was able to lay low enough in the water to endure the storm. Every young sailor hung onto something. I imagine my nineteen-year-old father hung onto that Navy Prayer Book and prayed to this Jesus whom he tried to worship each Sunday in an incense-filled two-hour church service. The rough seas and howling winds were unimaginable. They were tossed like a ping-pong ball back and forth for twelve hours in the narrow confines of a ship's bowels.

All wars end and time begins to fly. The GI Bill affords college. A pretty new wife is found. Two new kids join the family. A good home in Brookfield, Wisconsin. Postwar America provides unprecedented business opportunities. The Armenian Church plays a guiding role. Still, there is a striving of the soul for more. There are deals to be made, card games to play, and football games to attend.

Demos Shakarian, one of the most successful dairy farmers in all of California, was called to be an evangelist to the common businessman. He would begin the Full Gospel Businessmen's Fellowship International (FGBMFI) in 1953. It would reach men worldwide. Demos and his family had the largest private dairy farm in all of California in the 1940s. In his famous book, *The Happiest People on Earth*, Demos relates how his family lived in Armenia and were Pentecostal Armenian Christians. This would mean they believed that the Holy Spirit healed people and had prophetic messages not just in biblical days but even today. One of those prophetic messages came from a Russian Christian boy who proclaimed a coming massacre of Christians. The Holy Spirit had given him this message. A calamity was coming to Christians in that village. Somewhere around 1908, that illiterate boy would draw a map of the United States and would tell the villagers to go to the west side of this vast country and resettle there. This, in itself, was a miracle as the boy would have no way of knowing what world geography looked like, let alone choose a coast to go to. Those who believed in these prophetic messages of Holy Spirit guidance believed his message. They left the villages! Those that did not sadly were slaughtered by the coming Armenian Genocide. Taking the three-month voyage, these Armenian believers, including the great-grandparents of the famous Kardashian clan, settled, bought and worked farmland in the San Joaquin Valley, Fresno, San Jose, and other prime areas in California. They became multimillionaires over the generations and were blessed beyond belief.

Demos tells the story in his book of how he and his father would come to cow auctions in Oconomowoc, Wisconsin. They would be competing against iconic families like the Pabst Brewing family (Pabst Beer). Each would have to bid on the best cow that could produce the most milk. Demos and his father always chose the finest milk producer. One day the Pabst family inquired about their technique.

Their response was, "We listen to God. He tells us which one to buy." The Pabst brothers did not follow the conversation.

The Full Gospel Business Men's Fellowship International was started with that dairy money.

This was a charismatic, Pentecostal-inspired organization that ministered to businessmen. They were men who wouldn't step into a church, men who delegated church activity for the family to their wives. Men who could command the respect of 100 employees but could not come face to face with the God who made them. Men who were janitors and knew their place amongst other men. Men who found solace on a bar stool where they would not be judged by the words that came out of their mouths or the clothes on their backs. Men who owned one pair of shoes and other men whose wealth actually kept them away from God. Men who lived double lives with mistresses. Men who treated their wives poorly. Some were skeptics about everything in life. Some still had nightmares from their war years. Some had drinking problems, some just felt too dirty to face a Holy God. Who would bring a balm for their souls?

Jesus called Demos to seek these men out.

Demos hugged all of them. He embraced them with this simple message a child could understand:

"Jesus loves you as you are. You cannot bring any righteousness to Him. He knows your sin; He knows your heart. He gave Himself for you and offers a new beginning in Himself for you. He will bring you rest and peace. Just knowing these things is not enough. You must take the step to ask for forgiveness and invite Him into your life. Don't try and change and then come to Him. He will take residence in your heart and change you from within."

For me and millions throughout history, that is the 2000-year-old Gospel message.

And it worked! Men brought other men. CEOs of Fortune 500 companies sat next to the janitor or factory worker for a Saturday morning breakfast at some chain restaurant. No fancy church buildings or decorative halls. Plain and simple back rooms of restaurants. Song sheets were passed around, and these men, some who had not been in a church since they were children, well, they began singing, "It is well with my soul," "How Great Thou Art," mostly off-key. Then a car dealer would stand up and give a "testimony." He would explain how Jesus changed his life from within once he surrendered all to Him. They were told that they should be an example and not neglect being the spiritual leader of the family. They were told to be Christian bosses and Christian workers. To bring their new understanding of Jesus's love for them into their workplaces. To not cheat your boss. To treat your wife with respect and love. To love your children. To be a good boss and not provoke your employees. Some men had tears. Others lifted their heads high for the first time. Some hugged other men. Having attended some of these, you could almost sense the beating of angel wings above this ragtag group of men.

"How about you, Nazar? Have you given your life to Jesus Christ?" said this Demos as he stood looking down at my dad. Bald like my father but with snow-white bushy hair and full frizzy Armenian eyebrows, he waited for my father's answer.

My dad would never come to some event like this. Many times, he would explain to my mom, "I go to the Armenian Church. All these guys are after is money; I knew a fellow who read the Bible and jumped off a bridge and killed himself."

He fought tooth and nail to avoid these "religious" gatherings.

But Mom knew better. She said, "Nazar, there is the ARMENIAN guy who is going to give a Christian message. He is a multimillionaire. I think you might want to hear him."

An Armenian guy? Well, what is wrong with that? And a multimillionaire? Okay, let's go. He had, after all, seen a change in my mom. She no longer argued with him and showed a love that they had when they were first married. All because of a Bible study? Come on?!

So there Nazar found himself, right up on the small platform with this extra-large-chested, tall Armenian asking him the question.

"Well, Demos, my wife goes to prayer group every Wednesday, and the ladies pray in tongues and read the Bible."

"That is wonderful. And you, Nazar?" Demos asked.

"Demos, my daughter went to a Billy Graham rally and now goes to church regularly and studies the Bible. So does my son."

"Nazar, you have a blessed family. You must make your own decision. You may know a plane will leave New York and arrive in Milwaukee, but until you actually get on that plane, you will not get home. Would you like to surrender your life and ask Jesus to bless you by allowing His love into your life?"

I was there; I saw this, I heard it. I had heard of a time when his grandmother, whom he had never met at the time of her death, passed on the generational Hajinian family blessing to his mother. Would that blessing again come to fruition? My father's face took on a white countenance I cannot explain. Was I seeing things, or was there a lightness to his face and head? This man was never a bad person, lived a fair and good life. Certainly, he had his issues and personal sin, as we all do. He was not a good dad; he was a great dad. His life was spared in the metal hull of a ship in the Pacific. At this moment, he remembered or forgot all the wrong he had done. The lies, the cheating, the ashamed things we all hide and run from. They came to the surface. A silent spiritual confession took place.

Face shining, he said, "Yes. Demos. I want to give my life to Jesus."

I don't specifically remember the prayer my father prayed at that moment. But it was not the words but the attitude of the heart that mattered. When you submit yourself to God, you might think it is business as usual, but God's love pours into your heart, and you begin to live a new life and, in some ways, unknowingly. Tears flowed down my sister Patty, my mom, and my cheeks. We came up and hugged both dad and Demos. My tough dad, the Navy guy, was biting his lower lip to keep the tears from forming in his eyes. It didn't work.

The changes we saw in our great dad would fill pages. Before, he was a great dad. Now he was to become the man God always wanted him to be. Suffice it to say, the employees at his leather factory asked him why he didn't yell at them when they made mistakes or missed deadlines, or were late. His response was always the same. "I gave my life to Christ, and He has loved and changed me." Many didn't understand and thought it was a joke. Some laughed. None could deny he had changed dramatically.

Nazar, who loved people unconditionally before, now was a powerhouse of care and friendliness to all those he came across: strangers in elevators, neighbors, relatives. He and my mom were called to leave the Armenian Orthodox Church and serve in the Brookfield Assembly of God Church to serve out their remaining seasons of life. Changing the way you do things is never easy, especially when you are older. There is comfort in repetition, in the old ways. But God is a creative God. Comfort is not always on His list for us, but a full and blessed life is, and sometimes for some people, that means a change in churches. At their new church, they found the tools to help others find faith and love in Christ.

Nazar would go and see his friend in Christ, Demos, each time he would come to town. He also took me to the Saturday morning Business Men's Full Gospel meetings in the back of some 1950s restaurant. These men were from all walks of life. Some were wealthy, good-looking fellows, some were broken men, some were old and retired, worn down by a lifetime of work. All came to be inspired and sent out as an army of love. Jesus's love. To bring that love to all they met. These were Holy men. Not in a religious sense, but in a salt-of-the-earth sense. I was glad to be amongst them. Dad was truly enjoying himself.

Demos would be called home in 1993, but the FGBMFI continues and is celebrating its seventieth anniversary this year.

When asked how things are going at the Assembly of God Church, the old Navy Nazar would pipe up, "We are busier than hell!" he would declare. Everyone loved my dad. To this day, I get stories of his faith and that of my mom.

Our arms are too short to box with God. He wants us to know He loves us. He created us. He is providing the blessings we have. He will tap each and every one of us sometime in our journey on this blue-green marble we call home. For some, it will be as a child, others as a teen, some in our forties, and others in the fall or winter of our lives. Be sensitive to that tap. Look for it. It is why we were made.

Nazar would meet his Savior in October of 2009.

Double Vision Correction

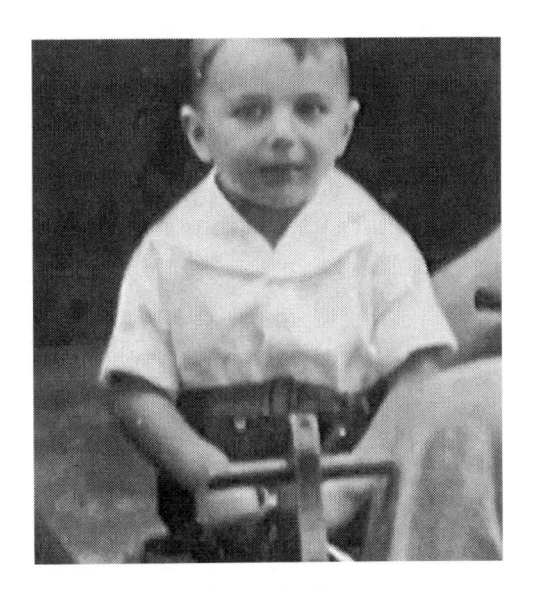

Author, age five, before surgery

Standing next to my hospital bed with the guard rails up, my mom leaned over and kissed my five-year-old forehead.

"Tomorrow morning, the doctor will fix your eyes, so they don't cross. I will be there right after the surgery." Clutching her shiny thin black leather purse, my mom turned and walked out of the darkened room, leaving her five-year-old son to find sleep in the dark night of a hospital room. The only light came from the hallway through a frosted glass half door.

This was not a single room. It was a room filled with beds of children who were getting ready for surgery the next day. Sheets rustled as the children began to try and climb out of their pen-like beds.

Mothers were now gone, and the loneliness and uncertainty were expressed in the sobs and crying that began to fill the air.

"Hey, don't cry. Everything is going to be okay, guys," I softly shouted to the wailing that was becoming a fever pitch of noise.

"It's okay. It's okay. Tomorrow, Mom will be back, and we will be all fixed up." Then even a little lie came out of my mouth. "Hey, we could maybe get some toys."

Slowly, the pain level began to drop.

"We need to go to sleep so the morning can come."

Whimpering levels continued to drop.

Soon, some began to fall asleep.

My last words bounced off the shadow-filled room floor: "Everything will be okay."

With an occasional whimper, I hugged my blanket and let some of my own anxious tears hit the pillow. I missed my mom. Sleep, like a warm, light snow, covered my thoughts, and I slept. Waking up with the morning sunrise spilling through the big windows in the room, I noticed that the streetlight right outside was still on. That, to me, was a mini miracle—I had gotten up so early that the streetlights hadn't been turned off, and yet it was morning. The guy who turns them on and off had not gotten out of bed. I was up before him!

Soon I was wheeled to a surgery suite, where I was given some red liquid to drink. It tasted pretty bad. Next thing, I woke up with a bandage over my good eye, and there was my mom and dad to take me home.

For the next six weeks, eight weeks—I don't remember—I wore a patch over my good eye. This was done so that I would use my bad eye and strengthen the muscles in the weak eye.

For those with a bad eye, and most people have a dominant eye, cover your good eye and try and walk around. My five-year-old frame would bump into things as I struggled to get where I had to go. Five-year-olds have energy. Lots of bumping.

Even though that surgery is outdated, perhaps even considered barbaric—weakening a good eye's muscles, so I use the bad eye to keep my eyes from crossing. It also confirmed that I have the great gift of encouragement. Tough times today? Things will always be better tomorrow. And if you cannot sleep due to tough times you face the next day, call me, but not too late. I will be going to bed early so I can be up before the man who comes around right after the sun comes up and turns off the streetlights.

Golfing with Dad Revisited

Dad would come home from work and take off his tie. It was 5:30, and we were going to the local public course for golf. I watched him methodically remove his work clothes and put on shorts and a golf shirt, leaving only his black socks to fit into his full leather golf shoes.

Dragging a forty-pound leather bag given to me by my uncle Hach, I struggled to get it into the trunk. Filled with old clubs from another uncle named Kay, I was ready to play. Golf was filled with life lessons for a thirteen-year-old. No fitted clubs for this kid. If it was good enough for an uncle, these clubs were good enough for me. And more important than your new club desires, they were free.

I learned patience from Dad. He told me that if I continued to swear as a thirteen-year-old, he wasn't going to play golf with me. I learned to swear from playing baseball in the alleys of Milwaukee. I was now living in Brookfield. A bad golf shot demanded a "damn it." Being a navy man in Pacific WWII battles, Nazar had heard his fill of cuss words for real reasons. Missing a putt did not qualify for uncivilized cussing.

Being with Dad, walking down the fairway, hitting the ball, no words were necessary. There is a bond—a son, a daughter—with a dad outside with nature. Hard to explain. Hard to put into words, so I won't try. My dad loved me without words.

Fifty years later, I play the same course. I come back home. Dad has long ago left this shadow-filled land for eternal sunshine. Two people's names are on the scorecard: mine and Dad's. I get a par on the first hole. So would Dad. Hole after hole. Dad walked and putted on these green fairways and flat and undulating greens, with his bow-legged walk, pulling his golf cart. I get a five. So does Dad. At the end of the round, I use my phone to take a picture of the scorecard. That image is immediately shared with ten friends.

The text reads:

"Playing golf at Greenfield Park with my dad in heaven—Chuck 48, Dad 48!"

My phone began pinging as a few tears hit the screen.

Summerfest in a Green Pinto 1978

I was sitting next to my dad, with his open-button summer shirt, behind the wheel of his lime green Pinto. "Narcotics. These kids are all on narcotics," my dad barked over his unlit cigar sitting in his mouth. Nazar was on a roll, surrounded by hippy teenagers and adults leaving a hippy concert on the shores of Lake Michigan. Our job was to find and pick up my seventeen-year-old sister.

Before cell phones or beeping locator chips, you set up things ahead of time with a paper map.

"Dad, pick me up on 3rd and Washburn at 8:30 on the Summerfest grounds, right on lake Michigan," my sister advised before she left that afternoon. The concert ended early, and waves of smoke were blowing off the lake—windows rolled down, we could not tell if the smoke was something burning or if it was tear gas. It could be tear gas as a mini-riot had taken place, and the cops were breaking it up. There were beads and bellbottoms, headbands, T-shirts, no bras, burning reefers, laughing, and singing.

"Narcotics. Look at these kids. They are out of control," Nazar said. We were blocked in with traffic on the Summerfest grounds. Right in front of us was a pickup with two hippy girls dancing. Arms over their heads, they were shimmying back and forth. Waving at my dad, he moved his head forward to get a closer look. They were flirting with my dad.

"What?" Nazar blurts out. Smoke was coming into the car as I scanned the crowds for my sister. The flirting and "come hither gestures" continued for Nazar. I was laughing inside while my dad grew the biggest smile on his face. He got it now!

All of a sudden, the Pinto was rear-ended by more hippy people from Illinois—bumper-to-bumper dents. No one was moving, so my dad got out of the car and met the Illinois license plate driver, who was obviously high, giddy, and laughing. My dad wrote down the driver's license and got back into the car. "Narcotics and dope, these dumb kids."

"There's Patty!" I shouted as I waved to my sister.

"Let's get out of here," Patty laughed as she threw herself into the back seat of the car. "They are starting a riot at the concert." These are exciting times.

We were going nowhere; traffic was stopped. "What's with the go-go dancers in the truck bed ahead?" Patty asked as she peered over the pinto bucket seats.

"They're flirting with your forty-eight-year-old dad," I laughed.

Eventually, we made it home. Dad told Mom, "These concert kids are nuts. Where are they getting all of these narcotics? At least I got the license number of this Illinois driver who dented the Pinto" He put his cigar, this time lit, back into his mouth.

The Illinois license was fake.

Mario 'Motts' Tonelli—
An Italian American
Survivor and Servant

Mario in 1941 and Mario in 1988, with second cousin Al Bianchi, whose son my daughter married.

The Japanese guard poked his metal staff into the stomach of Mario "Motts" Tonelli. Mario was too weakened after marching almost sixty miles as a prisoner of war in the Bataan Death March. The guard poked again, this time pointing to the gold ring on his finger. Motts had given up his freedom, his health, his professional football physique; he didn't want to give up this ring. A fellow POW reminded him that if he were dead, the ring would be useless. Slowly, he took off this piece of history. Perhaps he was thinking about what that ring represented or that game that allowed him to hold such a prize.

On a season-ending game in 1937, the Fighting Irish of Notre Dame met their bitter rival, the Trojans of the University of Southern California. Motts was the top fullback for the Irish, and with 40,000 people watching in the Notre Dame stadium, he scored the winning touchdown. His jersey number from high school to college to one year with the National Football League, Chicago Cardinals, was always 58.

Threatened by a severe beating, he handed the ring to his captor. His life was saved. Four years earlier, he was given the gold Notre Dame ring engraved with his initials and date of graduation after the College All-Star game. What could he do? For five months, he fought valiantly with Philippine and American troops. Running out of food, medicine, and ammunition, he was captured. Six hundred fellow American soldiers would die on the Bataan Death March alongside 15,000 Philippine soldiers due to beatings, lack of food, and unimaginable abuse.

Each day he would look at the ring and tell himself that tomorrow would be better. Now it was gone.

Or was it? The commander of the camp appeared shortly after the ring was stolen.

"Did any of my men take anything from you?" he demanded in perfect English.

Beaten and worn out, Motts replied, "Yes, he took my Notre Dame ring."

Lifting the ring up, the officer handed it back to Mario and explained that before the war, he had come from Japan and studied at the University of Southern California. He continued to tell the story about how he was at the game where Mario scored the winning touchdown against the Trojans in 1937.

"I know how much that ring means to you, so I want to get it back to you." He showed the only bit of kindness in over a year to this suffering prisoner of war.

Regularly moved from one prison camp to another, he saw over 1,600 of his fellow prisoners die. He would go from his football-ready 210 pounds to 98 pounds. Annals are filled with horrendous conditions and torture.

After over 1,200 days as a prisoner of war, enduring parasites, malaria, scurvy, and other life-threatening illnesses, he was transferred to a slave labor camp in Japan and given the number ... 58.

Through all the hard football practices, the crushing tackles, the cheers, the sports brotherhood, 58 was his identity.

That number gave him the boost he needed. It was his history; it was engraved in the ring he kept hidden.

"Boy, this is it. I know I'm going to make it now!"

As even evil itself burns out, enemies get tired. The war would end. Mario Tonelli would be liberated, and he would return to Chicago. Not having seen his wife, Mary, nor his parents and family for four years, his reunion could be described as the height of human emotion and relief. It had been after his 1940 professional football season that he enlisted to serve his country for what he thought would only be a year. His plan was to return to the Chicago Cardinals. World War II had other plans. So did the Chicago Cardinals, who didn't forget his service.

Too weak to resume a football career, the noble Chicago Cardinals put him on the 1945 roster for one game against the Green Bay Packers. This allowed him to get a football pension.

Continuing to serve his country, Motts served in local Chicago government in many diverse capacities. He finally retired in 1988. In January of 2003, he would be called to an eternal reunion with those whom he fought beside and gave the ultimate sacrifice.

Apples Falling from a Big Tree

Grandmother Tamom, six-year-old author, grandfather Haji Sarkis—1960

The 1960 White Ford Fairlane cruised down the new highway to Kansas City like a streamlined jet.

Families used to take vacations together—long before the current children that we have procreated became our universe. I mean, full families of grandpa and grandma too. Somewhere in the black-and-white universe of the past sat a six-year-old Chuckie Hajinian.

Wedged between my two non-English-speaking Armenian grandparents were Haji Sarkis Hajinian and Tamom Hajinian.

How I now love them so much and miss them. One of the reasons I am a Christian is that I believe when I leave this clay, there will be Jesus—no words spoken, and there they are with Him.

I digress. Armenian storytellers always digress. It is like putting salt on popcorn—a bit more enjoyable. More salt, please? Okay, okay.

Haji Sarkis—in 1913, he would make a trip from the Ottoman Empire (that had swallowed up Armenia) to Jerusalem. That pilgrimage made him a Mahdesi in Armenian—"one who faced death" (a trip to Jerusalem took you through some tough neighborhoods.) The Ottoman term was he was a "Haji." You put that before your name—you saw where Jesus walked, lived, and rose. That was your declaration and your badge. He was a slightly built man. His hands shook with age. They were separated from 1913 to 1920 (Another story, another time). In this story, they had been married for fifty-one years in 1960. Her name translates to Catherine or Patty. Beautiful Armenian names were squeezed and pushed with lots of pressure into an English equivalent. For example, Higanoush—Betty, Elsabet—Betty, Sironoush—Wilma. For men, Armen—Fred. After a while, I figured out the Americans were just using *The Flintstones* to replace these beautiful Armenian names!

Enough salt. Pay attention. I am wedged between my slightly built grandpa and my overly built grandma, wearing the typical blue dress with small white flowers splattered across the surface in a correct pattern. Her big arms with the wavy wings under her hidden biceps hugged the back of my neck. I am in the safest place in the world: protected by my grandparents. I will have to carry on their name, the name we have had for 800 years. No one knows. The church records were burned as the 400-year-old structures were leveled with incomprehensible anger in 1915. No other Hajinian male child heir exists. They know it; I am unaware.

In the front seat is my balding dad with a cigar in his mouth—not lit. Life is very good. He is with his family going to visit his brother's family. This is the Hajinian family Super Bowl. The red foamed console of the Ford Fairlane separates the other bucket seat where my mom sits. Only she has my two-year-old sister on her lap when she is not sitting on the foam console. Car seats for kids—whose idea was that? Seat belts were just coming out, and the fog of the moment did not allow a report. These are steel cars! "Just don't get in an accident" was the mantra of the day. Saved a lot of money on car seats.

So, what do Armenian grandparents who don't speak English do in the back seat of a car for eight hours? They eat! Come on, are you guys that dumb? Yes, they peel cantaloupes, cut up apples, peaches, pears, and, you guessed, chunks of a small watermelon.

"You take 'em up," my grandpa tells me in his broken English, as he rolled up the elbows, long-sleeve white shirt displays his only tattoo" "1913," his Haji-Jerusalem pilgrimage birthday.

"Pass the watermelon to your father," my mom says with a big smile.

Dad takes the cigar out of his mouth and puts it in the ashtray on the shiny front panel of the dash with one hand on the wheel, reaches back, grabs the watermelon, and begins eating it while his dutiful wife awaits and wipes his chin with her long-stretched arm over her daughter Patty's head sitting beside her in the bucket seat. Oh, they had their marriage battles, but this time, she lovingly keeps the watermelon from dripping so he can concentrate on the road.

After eating the watermelon, pears, apples, and every other fruit known to mankind from the time of the Romans right up to 1960, my dad makes a warning announcement. Announcements play an important part in every Armenian gathering. It can happen at any time during the party. You better not be in the bathroom. "What did he say? I missed it. Yeah, you missed it. Too late." It is like someone giving exit instructions during a fire. Everyone is called to shut up and listen. It is the power move. It is the, *I may be ugly, not too bright, not very wealthy, but I know this which you don't, and that makes me a bit higher on the food chain than you are!* It is a marvelous game!

Some salt now. For example, our cousins love it. "Someone says Saran Wrap caused cancer, so don't use it to cover your food, and for God's sake, don't use it in the microwave." We burst out in laughter as this serious cousin starts blinking her eyes real fast. We are not buying this latest *I know something that you don't, and thus, if medals were given, I would get one.* Laughter turns to argument while we eat chips and peanuts. Great, great times without cable television.

"Don't ever, EVER, throw anything out the windows. There is a $100 fine for littering, and I saw a police car a mile back," my dad warns us with his big brown eyes flashing warning signs in the rear-view mirror. Armenians don't like to give up hard-earned cash, especially for some rule that they did not invent.

Count—one, two, three, four … Eyes gazing off the road for a moment and back into the rearview mirror, my dad, Nazar, wait for it … sees a bag of garbage—watermelon chunks, apple cores, cantaloup skins, napkins … hit the windshield of the car behind us, spraying our leftovers all over the road.

Nazar explodes, "Chuck, I just told you not to throw things out the window." Looking above my eyeglasses falling off my then-small nose, I do the six-year-old bent elbow—I point to grandpa. I had to give him up.

"Pa, what the heck are you doing?" my dad says, still looking in his rearview mirror, hoping his car stays on the road while the car behind us keeps spraying windshield wiper fluid.

Grandpa Haji Sarkis, the guy who fought with the vastly outnumbered French Foreign Legion to free Palestine from the Ottomans, who had a 1913 tattoo, who never saw his mom, brothers, or sisters after 1913 or witnessed their deaths in 1915, who loved me without words, my hero, says in full Armenian:

"Are you *KHENTEH* (CRAZY)? You expect Garbo (me, "Chuck" in Armenian) and me to sit in the backseat for five hours with all this garbage?"

Inch es, Khent es? Goozes vor hing jham yedevuh nsdink ays hodadz aghpov? Turs nedetsi

"What are you crazy? You want us to sit back here for five hours with this smelly garbage? I threw it out!"

Grandma and my mom burst out laughing. Life is very good.

A Surreal Circle Surrounding Susan

"You are my older sister, Susan. God loves you. You will get you through your divorce from Jordan." So says my sister Beth, with tears in her eyes. Why would either of them care? She never liked my Jordan, even after our ten years of marriage. As for God, who loves someone when they are kept in the deep corners of the past?

I just don't want Jordan anymore! I can feel the hot sand between my toes as we walk on the beach of the French Riviera.

"Jordan, why are you ten feet ahead of me?"

These French women with their tops off, big, heavy French women. Jordan does not even notice.

"Jordan, what are you thinking? I am leaving you. Can you hear me?"

I am a Vassar girl. We do what we want. East Coast, our own rules.

"Slow down. Do you hear me? Jordan, why are you leaving me?"

For ten years, we had the best of conversations. Our families got along. Remember the month we rented the fifteenth-century cottage that was used as horse stables in Aix-en-Provence? We were a stone's throw from Renoir's home at Les Colettes. The jewel-colored Mediterranean inspired some of our best lovemaking. This was heart and soul. Sea and salt filled our nostrils. We lost our identity, our self-consciousness in each other's arms.

Why do I want to give this up? I want to feel my legs move. My eyes can't see them.

"Jordan, wait up for me. Can you just wait up?" I can't walk in this thick sand. I disappeared in your love. Where did all the people go? We were just on the beach. For ten years of marriage, we have been on the beach. I am so sensitive yet dulled.

"Why must you need happiness to be happy with me?"

That sun is blinding.

"Turn around, Jordan. Show me your chest; show me that blond hair that drove my sorority sisters nuts. I am losing you in this fog; why is it now raining? My thoughts are bending to my emotions. The water is taking me, do you care? I hate you, Jordan; I HATE YOU!"

"Hey, hey, HEY! Wake up, Susan. You are having a screaming bad dream! Wake up. You have your final exam at 10 today."

"What? What dream? Jordan, how old am I? What are you talking about?"

"You are exactly twenty-two years old, and if you plan on graduating from Vassar in two weeks, you better get that cute rear end out of bed and take your final exam."

Vini Orlandini, The Tattooed Man, Has Died

I first met Vini when he brought his seventy-five-year-old mother into my medical office for care. She was a slight woman with a quiet demeanor. A gentle, slow smile revealed a hint of dementia.

Vini was just the opposite—a large-figured, gregarious man about 5 feet 9 inches. Close-set eyes hid behind black factory safety glasses from the 1950s. His full cheeks always sported a day's beard growth long before it became popular. Even in his mid-fifties, his hair was jet black with slight thinning at the temples.

One day, after bringing in his mother, Vini asked to be seen for a checkup. Patients are patients. Each day brings new ones, and few are remembered or noted. Vini was different. On each finger, he had a tattooed symbol. Going up his arm was the face of a jazz singer whom I had never heard of. I came to learn Vini loved music. And tattoos. This, of course, took place in the late 1980s to early 1990s, long before tattoos became the attention grabber and the soon-to-fade vogue sign of personal uniqueness for those seeking an audience.

Every year, Vini would show up with his mom.

"Hey, doc. Look at this one," Vini would say as he rolled up his short pants and showed off two new tattoos on his thighs.

"Glenn Miller here. He died flying on an airplane to entertain the troops during World War II in 1944. And Woody Herman and his clarinet here. He was born in Milwaukee," Vini proudly exclaimed.

Damn, sure enough, right there was bespectacled Glenn Miller holding a baton, while Woody peered across the leg with his hands holding a clarinet in full color, spread out across and around the front of his thighs.

"Watch when I pull my skin how Woody looks like he is playing his clarinet," Vini chuckled.

These were the good times for Vini. Eventually, his mom would pass away. Vini's weight became a major health issue. Each year, more tattoos were added—a dragon going up the neck, more symbols on his hands, and famous midcentury big band players of a lost era—well, they got bigger!

Vini was now in his sixties, and he needed his heart medicine. He would confide in me that he could no longer pay for his medicine, let alone the heat for his home. He began to look ragged. I was able to get a decent Medicare plan for him and gave him heart medicine samples.

"Vini, there are organizations to help you pay for your heat," I would tell him. "You can't live in a house in a Milwaukee winter without heat."

He'd just smiled and turned away.

The years came off the calendar with Vini stopping in for his checkup and me reminding him that his weight gain and high blood pressure were not good.

"Who's gonna show off Woody and Glenn if you don't take care of yourself? And your knee may need replacing soon," I would tell him matter-of-factly.

He would respond that his roof was now leaking snow, and he confined himself to the kitchen, with heat coming from his stove. The neighborhood had gangs roaming around with gunshots at night. He was afraid to go out. He didn't know how to sell the time-worn house he had shared with his mom his whole life.

Summer led to the fall, and the drop in temperatures sent a sharp chill to the body. The darkness of winter had arrived.

"Hey, remember Vini the Tattoo guy?" my office manager Sandy asked.

"Yeah," I said as I stopped typing in some patient's chart.

"Well, he died two days ago. Here is the obit," Sandy said, putting the paper in front of me.

ORLANDINI, VINCENT
Entered eternal rest on January 20,
Preceded by his mother, Carmella Orlandini.
Vincent was a former employee at Linemann Battery company. Visitation January 22 at Molten Dell
Funeral home 4:00-7:00.

As a doctor, I have obviously had patients die—old people whose life cup was full, some young ones who didn't deserve the quick ride into eternity. I sigh, sometimes say a prayer for the family, then coldly move on to the task at hand.

Vini's death was different. I couldn't get his lack of a story out of my head. What did I really know about this friendly oddity? I was curious as to who he really was. What was his life like? For the first time in years, I decided to attend a patient's funeral.

January is a horrible month to die. At 4 p.m., when you arrive at the funeral home, the sun is setting, and it's cold. And when you leave, it is dark and even colder. This time snow was added to the mix.

Molten Dell is one of those "old time" neighborhood funeral homes with the full billowing velvet curtains and religious pictures from the 1940s and '50s. A young Jesus with sheep. The Scandinavian Jesus with flowing light brown hair and clear blue eyes. A picture of Moses with his staff. The walls had multiple coats of paint or decades-old classic wallpaper. Nonetheless, it served its purpose.

I told the brown-suited attendant I was here for the Vincent Orlandini funeral. He guided me and held back the belted curtains that led to a small room with twenty chairs and the open casket holding Vini. Wall sconces dimly lit the room. I was hoping a relative or someone would be there. No one was present. I walked up and looked at Vincent. A slight smile, like I remember, was on his face. His tattooed hands were folded across his chest. I tried to make sense of the symbols. I finally had the time.

At that moment, I sensed someone behind me. My startled look made her apologize, "I am sorry to interrupt."

"No, not at all. Vincent was a patient of mine, I was his physician," I sheepishly said. "I really knew nothing about him."

"I worked with Vini at Lineman. My name is Tammy Orshesky," she revealed with a limp handshake.

"Dr. Chuck Midland," I said as we both stared at Vini.

"Would you like to get a cup of coffee? I really want to know more about this guy who I took care of all these years. I want to think of my patients as people—people with a history that I seldom get to know about," I explained.

"For example, I never asked him about those letters on his fingers."

Tammy turned her head away a moment and wiped a tear away. "Those letters on his fingers are the first letters of French towns."

More confused by her explanation, we both left to get a coffee at the Starbucks down the block.

"I don't mean to be rude, but I only have a few minutes for the coffee. Those letters are the French towns that his father fought and liberated in World War II," Tammy stoically explained.

"The obituary never listed a dad or any other relative," I stated.

"His mom's family were from New Jersey. She got pregnant by a GI heading over to Europe in 1943. Getting pregnant out of wedlock was quite a stigma back then. She had a distant relative in Milwaukee and was shipped off to live with her. Vini was born and raised by his mother and this relative. His mom worked for Gimbels Department Store designing displays for the windows. Vini was born in 1944, and they never heard from the father. Somehow, his mom heard through the grapevine that he might have died in 1944."

"1944?" I interrupted.

"Yes, his mom never said much to Vini about him. She just knew he was in the 82nd Airborne, Dragon Company. When he was growing up, she would tell Vini about the cities that were liberated by the 82nd. Never mentioned his last name, but his first name," Tammy paused, looked out at the streetlight-illuminated snow now hitting the coffee shop window, "his name was Vincent. Listen, I really have to go."

90

"Wait, one last question," I begged. "Why did he let himself go like he did? I told him there were hotlines to help him with heating his home, and he could have gotten money out of the house and moved to an apartment. Maybe I could have done more?"

"Doc, some people fight to stay in this world. Others are just tired. They don't want to fight anymore. The mind gets tired; the body fails even under a good doctor's care."

The house belonged to this unknown relative, then his mom, and finally, she left it to him. It was a rough neighborhood. He left the company on disability. His eyes were bad, and his legs could no longer support his standing. I would stop by to see him. He had no one, really. He lost his mom to dementia long before she died. Why would he want to stay in his breaking-down house and failing body?

"Don't get me wrong. He was not depressed. He just gave up," Tammy explained as she got up.

Not wanting her to leave, I clumsily followed her out and blurted, "And the tattoos were his hope and monument to his unknown dad going back to 1944?"

She nodded, as a distant smile mouthed her final words, "You got it, doc! Say a prayer for Vini."

Turning into the now-blowing snow, she disappeared as the wind whipped unseen ice particles into my face and down my neck. I covered my face and ran to my car.

Bedtime Stories for the Grandkids

This, of course, is a special time. Four grandkids, all under the age of six, are staying over, and there they are, tucked into their beds. Steve is wearing Spiderman pajamas. Peter, Nazar, Steve, and Polly are all settling in and waiting for the bedtime story. Looking down at them, they brush away the hair on their foreheads. Teeth are all brushed, goodnight kisses are given to Grandma. A full day of activities is taking its toll. Arms and legs stop thrashing around.

"Grandpa, you promised a story," Steve reminds me.

"Okay, what kind of story do you want?" I retort.

Peter is quick to blurt out, "Grandpa, we don't want stories about when our parents were kids or stories about God."

"Well, that about covers it all, I guess," I respond, taken back a bit. "What would you like to hear about?"

"Tell us about spaceships and planets!" shouts Peter from under the covers.

"Yeah, tell us about that kind of stuff," seconds Steve.

"Don't make it scary, 'cause my mom says I get nightmares if a story is too scary," announces Polly.

"How can you get nightmares from a spaceship story?" inquires Peter.

"I have to get a drink of water," announces Polly.

What is it about bedtime that makes kids get dehydrated? I realize I'd better start the story, or they will never go to sleep. So, I begin telling them about a book I wrote in the sixth grade about a spaceship and a planet that mined jewels. Questions began halfway through, and I had to make stuff up as I went. Of course, the questions continued.

"Grandpa, what kind of air did they breathe? Most planets don't have oxygen. How could they mine jewels with no oxygen to breathe?" Nazar inquires.

"Well, they had a special piece of gum that they could chew, and that gum changed the air to oxygen for them to breath," I quickly announced.

"That's dumb," responds Steve.

"I'm thirsty," announces Nazar.

"There are no monsters, I hope, 'cause my friend Vivian, well, she heard a story about monsters and got nightmares," reveals Polly.

The questions began to slow down, and the story slid on and on.

"The jewels were packed into the spaceship and brought back to Earth to make engagement rings. Since there were so many jewels, engagement rings suddenly became much cheaper, and the women's hands got bigger because they had to haul around these heavy rings," I would explain as I watched the weight of their eyelids begin to win the battle of consciousness. I bored them into dreamland.

There is something about a sleeping grandchild. These tornados of energy. Constant motion, "Come on, Grandpa. Push me on the swing. Grandpa, throw the ball again. Let's all go down the slide." Running here, now there. Hardly eating, then more running and swimming. Now eyes closed. Sleep has taken over their tired legs and arms. Their little heads are resting. They have been fully captured, finally. The activity of life is now dreaming.

I pray for them. No words, just thoughts of God's protection and wisdom, that decisions made in the future will be rightly guided and blessed. And thoughts of thankfulness to be able to see such grandkids. To remember how their parents tucked a towel in the back of their shirts and suddenly became Batman and Superman. How their world was filled with make-believe days of living on the prairie or dancing on a world stage of their backyard. Now grown with lives of their own. In the magic of grandkids, they return full of energy and love. Only this time, I am not responsible for their behavior or upbringing.

Interrupting my melancholy Kairos moment is Grandma. "Come on, Chuck, your grown kids, are watching home movies downstairs, and they want to know who the guy is with the full head of black hair."

"Okay, in a minute," I reply,

Standing up and before leaving, as the moon sneaks its white light through the cracks in the curtains, I speak to the now deep-sleeping four, "Sweet dreams, my true inheritance, sweet dreams."

Quarantine #6: Numbers on Paper

A caveman makes a mark on stone. A line, another line, and one more—three sheep. The sheep run away, but the lines on stone survive for 10,000 years.

"It's supposed to be seventy degrees tomorrow," I said to my wife enthusiastically after enduring a cold winter.

"No, it is only going to be fifty-two, according to the weather wizards."

The Dow Jones had its biggest one-week rise in fifty years—9 percent. Two days earlier, it fell 12 percent. A half-million dollars evaporated from George's 401(k).

"I am sorry I can only hit the ball forty yards today," admitted my wife's stepfather as we played golf. "Karl, at eighty-four years old, many men would kill just to be alive," I replied.

Resigning herself to the inevitable, a young woman in my Weight Watchers class sobbed, "I gained weight." A scale number brought tears and resignation.

A number on a machine. A number on a piece of paper. A ring of burning candles on a cake. A four-digit number recording a year. Numbers from a bank website.

Numbers from a doctor's report.

Symbols on paper make us happy, make us sad, rob us of peace, confuse us, give us a piece of the pie.

My mom explained to me what happened in the Great Depression: "People jumped out of tall buildings and killed themselves when the stock market crashed during your grampa's lifetime long ago." My six-year-old mind asked, "Why did people jump out of windows?" She replied as she dried the dishes, "Their numbers on paper crashed."

Symbols on paper, stone, computers, register tape, driver licenses, the money we handle, a breast size, a pants size, our car engine size, our batting average, our golf index, the number of lost loves, the number of made loves. Symbols for the irrationally aware mind.

Freedom from numbers awaits your decision.

My Armenian Aunt Mary

"You have a very pretty face, but you are fat," this jet-black-haired aunt of mine would blurt out at some unsuspecting cousin. Eight of my cousins would be gathered seven times a year for holidays or picnic events. For sixty-five of her ninety-seven years, I was her favorite nephew.

Some people spend little time with aunts or uncles. They are related but are not involved in heart, head, or soul issues—neither when they were growing up nor when they themselves became old. Cousins would also be distant. The focus is on the immediate family. Relatives are a nuisance and an unwelcomed intrusion in a perfectly folded selfish napkin world.

My family was just the opposite. We had Aunt Mary, and she was a cannonball. The beauty of a "second opinion" on your life issues is that it makes you sit straight. It makes you evaluate your decisions from a self-centered, self-absorbed nature to one of *sometimes* wisdom. My aunt was in our lives weekly. We went to the same church. My parents had the same friends. My aunt felt it was her family duty to give advice at every turn. To right this ship called "The Life Journey."

"Lucy," she would tell my mom. "You have to keep these kids in line. People will talk!"

"People will talk" was probably something left over from the old country where they didn't have telephones or newspapers. People talked to everyone. "Did you hear that Anne's kid wore his shoes on the wrong feet when he went to school?"

"Doesn't surprise me. Have you ever looked at the kid's father? My father knew his father's brother, and they said his well was not too deep, if you know what I mean!"

Nowadays, no one cares what someone else's kid has done. "My daughter has five boyfriends, and she sleeps with all of them!"

"Well, at least she is popular, Susan. I really like the way your grass is so green, and it stands up when you mow it."

My aunt would stand up and say, "Are you nuts letting your daughter sleep with five men? Don't you know that most men are in the antiquing business, but they don't like used furniture?" Or some kind of retort like that. Believe it or not, she actually built up your self-esteem by knocking down your sandcastles.

There were sweet, shirt-off-the-back times also.

She was the aunt who bought me my first baseball glove when I was eleven years old. Before this happened, my father told my grandfather that I played a lot of baseball and could use a glove to catch the hard ball. My grandfather would walk the streets of South Milwaukee, and lo and behold, somehow, someway, a glove was left near the sidewalk, maybe touched the sidewalk, or at least cast a shadow on the public sidewalk—that must mean it is free. Sure enough, I got a big catcher's mitt that was made in 1909 and had a tiny pocket. It also weighed ten pounds and was for an adult baseball player from sixty years earlier, not a skinny eleven-year-old in 1965. In the Hajinian family, you never would spend money on sporting events or equipment. Need a hockey stick or a lacrosse stick? No problem. Grandpa can locate one. How about a jump rope? Simple. If grandpa couldn't find something on the streets of South Milwaukee, you simply changed sports. Aunt Mary buying me a baseball glove was a major game changer for the family.

Advice, lots of advice. I was thirteen years old at the time.

"Chuckie, don't be a dummy. Don't hang around with dummies, or you will become a dummy."

"Get a good education. Forget playing on the playground all the time. Study, get good grades, or you will become a dummy. No one wants to marry a dummy. You won't have a girlfriend, and you won't be married. You will end up a dummy."

All advice was followed up with a challenge to not be ignored.

She would qualify all her comments, "I am not the brightest or the smartest, but ..." Followed by "... Am I right or what? Tell me if I am wrong."

Of course, we would say, "You are right, Aunt Mary."

She would nod her head and say, "Yeah, see, yeah ... And another thing ... !!!"

There was always a gathering of the cousins, and when we were fourteen to sixteen years old, the lectures matured. Dating, sex, and *Playboy* discussions were on the menu.

"Chuckie, twelve seconds of pleasure can ruin your life!"

"Watch out for the girls; they will trick you, and you will ruin your life in five seconds."

I wondered what happened to the seven seconds of pleasure between the twelve and five seconds of the previous pleasure.

"Those women who pose for *Playboy* are nuts. Am I right? (My mom would be dusting the top of the refrigerator and nod her head.) Lucy and I would never pose for Playboy. I don't care how much money they offered!" she would proclaim with wide-open brown eyes blazing!

Turning to my cousin, I would say, "Did mom and aunt Mary really get a letter from *Playboy*? I hear it is good money, and geez, I could use a new bike!"

Life raced on for me. Aunt Mary was there, but I wasn't. The world caught my attention. Still, she was always the gift-giver, always the card-giver, always there, waiting for my eventual return. And return I did with a wife, a son, and three daughters. Gifts continued for each child—a piece of jewelry, a sweater, a card. It was nonstop love. What kind of aunt does that today?

We wanted to return the favors but were told by her, with stern warnings and pointed finger, "Don't get me anything; I have everything I need!"

We watched her age. Her jet-black hair would turn gray. Her sister, who was two years younger, always maintained a nice red-brown color even into her eighties. When we got the two together, which was quite often, we would tease them. "Why does Aunt Catherine have a nice red-brown hair color and yours, Aunt Mary, is white?" Here is the answer scientists have yet to discover: "Catherine drank milk growing up. I didn't," Mary would respond.

Age takes a toll, and Aunt Mary's eyesight and hearing faded.

She is legally blind, can't drive a car, but she knows if your belt buckle has been moved up a notch, you have gained weight, and she would let you know. No excuses like, "the dryer shrunk my pants."

"Chuckie, you need to lose weight," she would advise.

"I did. I lost ten pounds!" I would explain.

"Oh, you look good," she would admit, but not let you off so easy. "You need to take it easy. Don't work so hard. Money is nice, but it won't buy happiness. Your health is more important."

This thought would run through my mind, but I would dare not tell her. "Tell the phone company you won't be paying your bill, but you do have good health."

Pages and pages could be written, and someday they will. But for now, suffice it to say, this was a woman who, when I was four and had a fever, would come over and help my mom bring my fever down. During the late '50s, a common "medicine" was to give the kid a shot of whiskey. It would make the kid so hot that it would kill the infection. Aunt Mary also brought over aspirin. When my mom was ill with the flu, Aunt Mary would come over and do the laundry, cook, and take care of us. She would take us shopping. She would drive me to swimming lessons with my other cousins because my mom could not drive a car until she was thirty-eight. I think my aunt might have paid for those lessons, too, since my grandfather, no matter how talented he was in finding sporting goods, could not locate a pool for swimming lessons.

Fast forward to the deep winter of her life. Her husband, my Uncle Hach, would be whisked away with a heart attack while going to get the mail. She would spend twelve more years as a widow. We would tease her and ask her if she would consider marrying another man. She would raise her head, open her eyes wide, and exclaim, to our laughter, "Are you guys nuts?"

She spent many hours just sleeping in her assisted-living room, in her comfortable chair. She was cared for by her nurse daughter Nancy many hours a day despite being in a nursing-home setting and having round-the-clock care. She was well looked after.

The naps became longer. Then one day, I came to visit and again found her sleeping in her chair. My presence woke her, and she was about to talk. I expected a comment about eating vegetables instead of cookies, but instead, she said, "Chuckie, you cared for all of us. You came and visited."

It was like cold water on my face. My head went back. "You cared for us, Auntie Mary, our whole lives."

She simply and slowly nodded. Her hearing was gone. This time, though, I think she heard. Her arm holding the pointing finger slowly lowered to the edge of the easy chair. The next day, she took a long nap and slipped away, leaving us to fend for ourselves. But we are never alone. She left us with a lifetime of quotes and memories. She was ever so proud of our accomplishments and let us know that. I have tried so hard not to be a dummy. She was always glad about that.

I can hear her now, saying, "You don't need me anymore to tell you what to do. You are smart enough. Just get moving. Stop sitting around and take that cookie out of your mouth!"

Guilty Until Proven Innocent
from the book *Sandy and Garbo*

A book about our family yellow Labrador dog, named Sandy, written in 2007. Sandy the dog talks in bold *italicized print.*

Guilty? Me? I was fed whenever the Armenian relatives came over. This was a loud, confusing bunch. Some noticed me; others talked too much with their hands and feet. They almost stepped on me. One thing is for certain: they can pound down the food, and they drop a lot. When I lay in my bed late at night, I dream of people food. I am normally fed dried dog pellets made from some animal byproduct with a vitamin thrown in for nutrition. Think about eating the same dried dog food every day. These Armenian relatives were an easy stare-down for hustling food off their plates. I would sit in front of the weakest one of them and stare right into their eyes. My face would show no emotion but a cute, starving dog. If they didn't catch on, I'd shuffle my feet a little. Guilt would enter the picture. Soon enough, a cracker with delicious crabmeat would be dropped at my feet. Birthday parties are just great.

We Armenians are not big birthday people. Light a candle, sing a song, blow it out—let's watch the Packers. No major drama. Except today. This is the eightieth birthday of Aunt Mary, the matriarch of the whole extended Hajinian family. When someone considers it their job to give advice to everyone all of the time, we give them the title of matriarch. All of the Armenian relatives and their non-Armenian spouses were present. Uncles, aunts, cousins, kids, and even neighbors saw all the cars and stopped by to see what was going on. Lots of people.

Two large birthday cakes were sitting on the kitchen table. These were not your typical store cakes. These sheet cakes were so big they each had to be carried in a three-foot box. There they sat, smothered in chocolate frosting and candy sprinkles. Surrounding the cakes were the leftovers of a huge Armenian buffet. There were piles of food left over. Trust me, no one is on a diet. A diet is a period of starvation followed by a gain of five pounds. This crowd was stuffed to the gills. I told my wife that you can never run out of food when you have the Armenian relatives over. It would be paramount to insulting your parents or grandparents in front of their friends. You would truly be considered the village idiot. Their response would be swift and merciless. "Five people over for pork chops, and she only is serving five pork chops? Did a rock fall on her head when she was young? What is this Bah-Bomb?!"

When we were first married, Mary Kay would remark, "Wow, Chuck, can your relatives eat!"

What a great compliment. Compounding this great leftover food pile was the fact that everyone brought enough food to feed a small village. Rule number two: never come to someone's house for dinner without bringing more food than you and your family could possibly eat. That way, no one can say, "These people ate all of our food! Don't they have manners? They should have eaten something BEFORE they came over for dinner.

This is a tough crowd. They jostle for position in Mary Kay's kitchen. Secretively, hips bump hips until Mary Kay is edged out of the control position in her kitchen and my aunts are ready to serve. They hold the high ground in front of the sink, stove, and serving trays. Mary Kay gets to stand in front of the toaster. Sounding like street merchants, the servings usually went like this:

"You have to try my rice pilaf," my aunt Catherine would shout.

"Take two of my cheese *bourags*, Chuckie," another aunt would demand.

A cheese *bourag* is light pastry dough filled with brick cheese, butter, and some tiny pieces of parsley to serve as a vegetable. The whole thing is deep fried and absolutely delicious. I would explain to my aunt that I have high cholesterol and am taking medication. Cheese is not part of my doctor's plan for me.

"What do those doctors know?!" countered Aunt Catherine.

"I know of more people who have lost their hair from all of that cholesterol medication!" another relative chimes in.

Armenians know everything about every kind of medication. Well, no, that is not entirely true. They know someone who takes that medication and has a list of side effects for each one. And doctors? Unless my aunts hand-pick them personally, the whole bunch are just interested in money-making and unnecessary tests.

Why fight it? I take two cheese *bourags*. My aunt is happy.

When dinner is finished, we all retreat to the family room to watch a ball game and talk about life issues. For instance, "Whose family had the most money when they came over from the old country eighty-five years ago?" Stuff like that. We are happily bloated.

Soon the noise level reaches the same level as Lambeau Field when the Green Bay Packers score a touchdown. True to Armenian form, everyone is talking. Allow me to clarify that statement: everyone is talking at the same time. A question for the ages: When everyone is talking, who does the listening?

We Armenians have mastered that gift. We have the ability to figure out what you will say before the words leave your mouth. If we find the conversation interesting, we will listen. If we could care less about the point you are about to make, we simply ask you a question that may or may not be related to what is about to come out of your mouth.

Sound confusing? Here is a typical example. My cousin tells his uncle about his gallbladder surgery. The uncle simply has no interest in that surgery because he didn't have his out yet and instead wants to share HIS story. So, he simply changes the subject to something that he hopes interests my cousin so much that he will not be aware of the verbal slight that has just occurred. Here is how it plays out.

My cousin corners someone and explains, "I just had my gallbladder out, and boy ..."

Interrupting, my uncle shouts to him, "Hey, how about those Cubs? Are they gonna win the pennant this year or what?"

"You're crazy! Those Cubs are going nowhere this year!" my cousin responds.

Thus, my uncle wins.

Another warning about my Armenian relatives: they speak the truth whether you want to hear it or not. They will also give you the shirts off their backs. When one of my cousins lost her job, my father offered to make their house payments. Yet along with that love comes the frankness of their words.

My Uncle Kay hits my stomach and tells me that I've got to tone up. I look "heavy" to him. Uncle Kay has had problems with his eyes for over thirty years. He no longer drives a car, but he can tell that I have one more belt loop exposed. I immediately bring up the Cubs and Brewers, and he starts ranting about baseball. I walk away from the conversation and get lost in all the endless chatter that surrounds me.

These are schizophrenic conversations. "So-and-so did this. Where did they get money for that? Oh yeah, in the 1930s, their parents had a tavern." Apparently, if your grandparents had a tavern in the 1930s, you were set for life. There must have been hidden trust funds galore. This was simply due to the heavy drinkers in Wisconsin.

When we have a point to make, we simply talk louder and point a finger at the other person. We laugh, we insult, we show them who's boss! Aunt Mary pulls me aside and tells me that she always tells off her sister and my father, her brother. "I tell them off and put them in their place. Am I right, Chuckie? Before I can get an answer out, she looks at the heavens contemplatively and answers for me, "If I don't tell them off, who will?"

I guess she has a point. This is Armenian family therapy—having a relative remind you of your faults regularly.

In some families, brothers and sisters might not talk for months. In my extended family, we talk with cousins weekly. This may seem foreign to a non-Armenian, but each relative truly cares for and loves each other. There is nothing more precious for an Armenian than a blood relative, especially when the world outside seems harsh and cold. Hugs and kisses are the norm. So is criticism. Anyone with sharp edges stops coming around or gets those edges rounded really quick. It's like *My Big Fat Greek Wedding* on steroids. Rivaling faith in God, the family is extremely important, and dogs are not considered family members.

My aunts are not crazy about dogs. One simple reason: dogs use their tongues as toilet paper. Cleanliness is more important than anything to Armenians. You could be an ax murderer who cheated on your husband, but if you kept your house clean, who could really fault you? After spending three minutes looking at our dog, a question would arrive on my Aunt Mary's eighty-year-old tongue: "How long will that dog live?"

"Mary, don't say that. He's a good dog," my seventy-eight-year-old aunt would scold.

"Catherine, I am not saying anything bad. I was just wondering how long they have to still care for him?" Mary speaks defensively.

Sandy accepted this explanation, even though they had her gender wrong. She showed her thankfulness by licking Aunt Mary's leg.

"Ohhh! Don't lick me, dog!!" Aunt Mary screamed.

Sandy sensed their disapproval and headed for the kitchen. When the talk continued, she found her way to the table. Putting her paws on the table and tilting her head, she was able to lick about a third of the frosting off Aunt Mary's birthday cake. Even though the whole Armenian clan was ten feet away, no one noticed Sandy's follies. They were too occupied with the deep conversations.

Not to worry. There was another cake on the other side of the table with a chair blocking its direct access.

Labs are a thinking breed. They are stubborn and will work for hours to get their way. Sandy analyzed the situation and simply pushed her frosting-covered nose against the chair and moved it. Quickly, she placed her paws on the table and began licking more frosting off the second cake.

Peter and Mary Kay enter the kitchen to get the cakes for the candle lighting. We could always tell if Sandy had done something wrong. Her head would be down, ears pulled against her head. She couldn't look you in the eye as her tail curled between her legs. She would walk very slowly, almost as if walking on eggshells. Sandy knew right from wrong. She just couldn't keep herself from getting into trouble. Food now, repent later—that was her motto.

"WHAT DID YOU DO, SANDY?" Mary Kay scolded as she scanned the kitchen.

Peter was the first to see the missing frosting. "What kind of cake is this?" pointing to the cleanly licked cake.

"Oh no, Sandy!" Mary Kay shouted. By now, Sandy had stopped moving, and her soft green eyes began to blink rapidly. Was she going to get a hit on her snout with a newspaper? She knew something was coming.

Stacy comes to her rescue. "Sandy, did you eat that chocolate frosting? Oh, you poor dog, are you hungry?"

Sandy's head perked up as she slowly unwound from the fetal position. Her tail even managed to wag ever so slightly. *UM food?* She thinks, forgetting about her just committed trespasses. Mary Kay is furious with Sandy as Peter dumps both cakes in the trash. She is also worried about the effect chocolate has on the health of dogs. Their hearts can race, causing serious problems.

"I'm going to tell the relatives what YOU did," Sarah scolded Sandy.

Peter goes and breaks the news to the family as laughter and "oh no's "come out of the family room. Sandy escapes Mary Kay's wrath by following Stacy to her food bowl.

"Good, Sandy. It's not your fault you ate the cake," purrs Stacy. She pets Sandy while she eats a bowl full of dog food.

Stacy was always the one to sneak treats to me. If I had a will, I would leave everything I own to Stacy. Of course, I own nothing. I sleep where I want and use their blankets. I don't even own a food bowl. But Stacy has a dog's heart. She understands. She'd given me anything I wanted. ... Well, everything except chocolate cake. I had to get that myself.

We told Dave and Eddi what had happened. Laughing, they told us a story about their 120-pound yellow Lab named Dune. It seems that while everyone was occupied at their Christmas party, Dune put his paws on the table and ate every last cookie off the trays before they could be brought out for the guests. Still, to this day, Dave can get a guilty reaction out of Dune with the question, "Who ate the cookies?" Feeling remorseful, this huge dog will drop his head, pin his ears back, and tuck his tail between his legs. This occurs to this day, one year after the incident!

It has been proven that all Labrador dogs have a great sense of guilt. This is due to all the trouble this breed gets into. Great family dogs always come up with human characteristics. They have the daily wonderment of children. And like teenagers, they don't speak our language. Perhaps, Dune still remembers the taste of all those great Christmas cookies. They were too good to be legal.

After some quick thinking at the nearly ruined birthday party, Mary Kay found a small pound cake in the refrigerator and placed some candles on it. Turning out the lights, she brought it into the family room with all the fanfare of a birthday for the queen of England. Standing, we all sang with full, off-key voices, "Happy Birthday, Auntie Maaary." Not to be upstaged by guilt, Sandy came in and laid at her feet.

Chasing the Sunset

"Who is taking care of this man?" asked the doctor at the VA hospital.

"My mom is at their home," I replied with my good friend Dave at my side.

"Not anymore. He needs full-time nursing home care," the doctor stated authoritatively.

Unaware of the doctor's disappearing words, my father struggled to look up above his bushy gray eyebrows and simply said, "Thanks, doc."

The doctor, ever so moved, said, "Thank YOU, Nazar, for your service to this country."

Dave and I carefully helped him to his feet and, with the help of a walker, we got him back into the car for the ride back home. No words were said.

Settling back into his home of the past forty-five years, a conversation was explained to his partner of fifty-seven years. Mom, holding back tears, agreed to his move to a full-care nursing home. The dementia years had taken their toll on this warrior. Over a lunch worthy of a sequel in a Godfather movie, my sister and mom agreed it was time. I would take my dad to his final care facility.

Driving up, still, being sharp, Dad would ask," What is this place? Why are we here?"

I carry many DNA and social faults, but my one strength is encouragement. I reached deep inside and said, "Dad, we are here at this new place for you to live. There are all kinds of people who want to hear about when you were in the navy."

Without missing a beat, he opened his door and, except for the fact that he didn't know how to get out of his seat belt, he would have fallen right out. Telling stories is a Hajinian lifeline. He had willing people who would listen. Let me at them. He had to wait for me to come around with his walker and free him—like releasing the greyhounds at the racetrack to chase the mechanical rabbit. Click, off we went into the Happy Place. Greeting him were two black nurses: one tall and statuesque with an aquiline nose and one short with a round, beautiful smile and big arms. "Welcome, NA-ZAAR," they chimed.

Dad looked up. He sensed their love and followed them to his room as I brought in the only possessions he needed: seven shirts, seven underwear, and seven pairs of pants. Seven. The complete number of things. Two pairs of leather slippers, two pairs of sneakers, and three pairs of full leather shoes. Being the vice president and owner of a large leather tannery, he would never wear or allow his family to wear anything that wasn't leather.

"See the paper in the insole of the shoe you just bought? That's junk. What did you pay for these?" began the inquisition.

"Forty-five dollars," I would remark.

"WHAT?? Take them back. They are junk. Didn't I tell you leather insoles? They breathe, and your paper insoles are useless. You might as well put newspapers in your shoes," he would remind me.

"I can't take them back. I have worn them for two weeks," I pleaded.

"You guys just don't listen," he would say as he shook his bald head side to side.

Some kids would get corrected for not doing well in sports or school; we got corrected for not buying shoes that were 100 percent cowhide. We were to wear no plant products in shoes.

And so, it was time to say goodbye. "Dad, this is where you are going to live now, and these nice ladies will take good care of you. They want to hear your navy stories."

Looking up at these two angels, one with her arm around dad, he whispered to me, "I would like to go home."

"This is your home, Dad. This is Brookfield," I choked out.

"This is Brookfield?" he asked.

"Yes," I answered.

"Okay," he said.

It was time for me to go.

Sometimes emotions cause the body to freeze. You just can't make your body kiss him on the forehead or shake his hand. You can only turn and go. You remember the stories before you were born. How when they called his name to get his high school diploma, he wasn't there in the auditorium. He was in the bowels of a ship fighting the Japanese like a million other young American men. Most had never been an hour's drive from home. Now they were thousands of miles away and without their moms and family, facing death each day. How he ran a successful company, being part owner and getting only two weeks of paid vacation a year. How he raised two kids who introduced him to seven grandkids and one great-grandchild. Every restaurant meal was the finest he had ever eaten, and "you need to go there and try it right now—get in the car." How he lived his Christian life each day. We call that full circle. As I was walking to the exit, the statuesque nurse caught me. "Your father wanted to tell you something before you go."

Coming back, there was my dad, sitting on the edge of the bed.

Lifting his time-worn head, with a slight smile on his face, he said, "Thanks for everything you've done for me, Chuck."

I would be a liar if I said the floodgates did not open. The beautiful part of being human is to lose control, to really let go and let life's river carry you. I nodded and pressed his head to the bottom of my chest for a long time. Finally, I turned and walked out, not daring to dry the tears welling up inside my eyes. Reaching the car, I looked right into the setting Brookfield, Wisconsin, sunset and said, "Thank you, Dad."

The Persistence of Memory

A group of Armenian Girls who escaped from the Turks and sought refuge in Russia. Some of them are the only remaining members of their families.

A flashback hits my brain as I drive along the I-94 highway. The familiarity of driving for so many years allows this. Like singing to no one, my mind is writing a story to myself. It is enjoyable. For sanity, I share it.

Some fifty years earlier, I was seventeen on a hot July day at an Armenian church picnic at a county park. I am pinky dancing with all the eligible ladies my age. This is the circle dancing where your pinky hooks the pinky of the person next to you. Male or female, you move the left foot, then the right foot in a short forward kick, then take two steps to the right and repeat. It is simple. All shapes, sizes, and mental capacities—all are included. Some, however, can't get the right then left kick forward and just simply shuffle forward two steps. That is okay. We are glad you are here.

Sometimes the pinky you hold begins "punching in a circle," and your hand has to go along with it. You are held, hostage. Hands and feet, a Middle Eastern beat: clarinet, doompeg (Mideastern bongo), and the oud, a large mandolin with a long skinny neck and a giant watermelon belly. They reverberate in sound that cuts across thick cultures and time. It's a song with words no one understands. But this we know: for hundreds of years, the Armenians have danced to it. The sound is nothing most Americans have heard. The smell of the barbecuing lamb shish kebab wafts through the dancers. This is the food of the ancient kings. This intoxicating smell only adds to the Oriental swirling of these mysterious seventeen-year-old girls.

The car in front of me is slowing down without warning. "Did you ever hear of a turn signal?" I shout to the driver from inside my sealed car. "Where do these guys get their driver's license? The Dollar Store?" I speed past him.

My thoughts drift back to the dance and the stoic boy-men fighting to hold back the unbridled hormones deep within. The picture unfolds: full-eyebrowed girls, shadowing deep-set sparkling eyes, big smiles, tossed dark hair, and sandals kicking—all laughing coyly. Sweat is rolling down their foreheads and apple cheeks as the rhythmic sun beats down on us.

Each repeating circle dance brings me face to face with a group of old, seated ladies. They are the Q-tips—the white-haired grandmas. My grandma Tamom sits in the center, in control. These are big women to me. They wear full navy blue dresses with big polka dots or tiny flowers in the hot summer shade, their gray hair pulled into a convenient bun. They are indeed happy. Not one ever sought professional counseling for what they witnessed. They have each other. They watch, they smile, they point and matchmake. Then they laugh. Before them is their reward. You can read their past through their wrinkled eyes. This scene reminds them of their own youthful zeal, the small village butterflies of their youth some sixty years earlier.

They remember.

Cars begin swerving in front of me. Someone had a lifejacket blow out of their boat-in-tow, four cars ahead. I barely miss it. What kind of idiot just throws lifejackets into a boat without tying them down? We are on the highway at high speed, for cryin' out loud.

The dance comes around again. There are the Q-tips face to face with me. The circle is complete despite what my grandmother experienced at the tender age of twenty-two. She had been separated for seven years from her husband in a refugee camp in the deserts of Syria, not knowing if this day would be her last. Fifty years later, she watches her grandson, one of eight grandchildren born under her watchful eye. He is kicking his legs; he is noticing the girls. That is good. We will continue.

I remember.

Intro to Diets:
I Am Just the Way I Look Now!

The following pages will address ways of overcoming your self-image and will make you no longer base your self-esteem on the way you look at any given week, day, or time of day. I will POSSIBLY address:

Your weight concerns, real or imagined: Who is the judge, and do they wear glasses?

Your self-image and the scale: If numbers rob you of peace, take out the batteries and put them in a nice watch. Maybe an Apple Watch.

Fat—So what? Really, is Hollywood knocking? Did someone just call looking for someone exactly like you or me, only ten pounds lighter?

Are 'muffin tops" coming back? I hope so. I have had them my whole life and didn't know what they were called.

Why did God make me this way? What trouble would you have gotten into if you were thinner? He knows.

There is nothing wrong with skinny people: God bless them. Just don't let me stand next to them in a photo.

Here you go.

Part 1:
Creating the Illusion of Being Skinny:

I know I caught your attention—not with the word illusion, but the word skinny. For some reason, we bought the lie that everyone needs to be skinny. Skinny good, roundedness bad. Excess roundedness, criminal.

Americans spend billions on diets, gimmicks, and fads every year. How do I know that? I don't; I just made it up, but it fits in with everyone I know. Allow me to clarify: I am not against getting healthy by dropping a few pounds. Go for it.

But let's enjoy our life and stop looking at a muffin top (rolls of "tissue"—it is not always "fat") as a bad thing! Sure, you might live a year or two less, but have you seen people at the end of their lives? Not a pretty sight. Lots of drooling, aches, and pains. Also, many of us had overweight relatives who ate what they wanted, were big people, and lived to be ninety-five years old. So, if they lost that weight, they would live to ninety-seven? They are now dead and in Paradise. Who cares about two extra years when you can enjoy a custard ice cream sundae with Reese's Pieces and cashews? Pay attention.

So, enough. I thought this Part 1 was about creating the Illusion of Skinny.

Okay, here you go. Part 1. Here is my observation after studying myself in the mirror: Most people are not heavy-looking. Their heads are too small for their bodies! Mine included! That's right, small heads accent the body and give a distorted picture. I knew a dentist for forty-three years who would see it all the time. Small teeth, small smile, fat head. He would put veneers on the teeth, and the teeth would become bigger, head suddenly came into proportion—the person looked thinner. He had people waiting outside the hallway to sign up. Eventually, someone found them attractive, and the dentist was invited to their wedding.

Let's look at other ways of making the head bigger.

1. **Big hair.** Big hair was big in the '80s. In fact, hair got so big that they had to pad shoulders to balance out the look. Big hair and big padded shoulders. You could hide a large rear end with that combination. So, grow your hair out. Do you want to diet or spend more time drying your hair? While drying your hair with the hair dryer, your free hand can eat a nutritious vitamin and yogurt bar—win-win.

2. **Tease your hair**. Puffing it up by back-combing, which snarls up the hair and gives it more body. Men too.

3. **Facial hair growth:** Grow out your sideburns. Men too. If you ladies can't do that, consider spit curls just in front of your ears. Big in the '70s. Sideburns, beards, mustaches, goatees—all mean a fuller face and thinner-looking thighs—trust me.

4. **Makeup tricks.** Ladies know all about this. I don't. But if they can hide a nose by putting rouge on cheekbones, they can surely make their face look bigger—thus more proportionate with their larger body. I think red lipstick works. Eyeliner and eyelid cover—especially aqua blue and also white lipstick.

5. **Accessories. Big hats.** The eyes are drawn from the belly to the cool hat the guy or lady is wearing. Be creative. Watch the Kentucky Derby. Lots of people who should be booked in a Weight Watchers convention instead of sipping mint juleps are wearing the most amazing hats—and admit it, they look pretty good. If I was in my thirties or forties and still living with my mom, I would marry one of them.

6. **In photos, make sure your head is in front of the others.** Also, do not stand at the sides in a photo. Get in the middle and move your head forward. People on the end will have small heads and distorted, large bodies.

Again, a win-win for you. That alone is worth the price of this book. Don't share. Make them buy their own book.

Finally, God made you the way you are. Rejoice in that we are all unique and built differently. We also were made to enjoy food. It's in the Bible! Do you want to disobey the Bible? Then you better finish that sandwich. Enough personal complaints. When we are disgusted with our body, in a way, we are not being grateful and are actually coveting that skinny model in *People* magazine who just eats crushed ice and Tic Tacs for lunch. All of which I believe is a sin.

You have a wonderful manner about you. You have an interesting personality, and you help people. Perhaps the skinny *People* magazine model and movie star do not. In the long run, what is more important?

Part 2: Work On Your Height, More Get-Thin Tips from Garbo

Get an **inversion table**. Get the kind that straps your ankles in—and go upside down. Make sure someone is there so that you can get back up. By stretching yourself, you will add an inch or two. This will allow your body to use up more height space, and you will naturally look thinner.

Put your head and shoulders back. Most of you are leaning forward like you are looking for a $20 bill on the floor. I have been looking for sixty years and have never found a $20 bill. So, for the love of God, put your head up and back! Okay, I have found a dollar crumpled up when I was thirty-five. And one time, while snorkeling—true story—I found $27 stapled to a restaurant tab. I had an underwater metal detector, but the cash was paper money. But is all that looking worth being shorter? No! Get a part-time job if you need the money. Put your head back while you read this and put down that Twinkie. Putting your head up and back—this will add two inches and keep your ears from rubbing on your shoulders. No one at the Goodwill wants sweaters with worn spots on the shoulders.

Wear lengthening clothes. Get opinions from others. Ask: "Does this turtleneck sweater make me look heavy?" Ask people. You know they are judging you already, even though they don't say anything. If they say no, that means you have the correct height. If they say yes, take it off right there and tell them they can have it since they are soooo skinny. Then act like it doesn't matter and leave. They will be the ones that will be confused. They are jealous anyway.

Be long-waisted. Pull your belt down lower. This will make you look longer from the neck down. If you do the opposite and wear your belt way above your belly button, right under your chest, you will look ridiculous, and people won't care if you are skinny.

Remember, God made you the way you are and gave you the ability to become what you want. Enjoy.

Part 3: Looking Thin Rather Than Being Thin, or Passing a Test Without Reading the Book

Fact: Liz Taylor always weighed the same throughout her movie career. She just changed the style of their clothes. For the millennials, Liz Taylor was a wonderful Academy Award-winning actress that the press followed around most of her adult life, publishing pictures of her weight gain and loss for people in the seventies and eighties who didn't have a hobby (before cell phones and Facebook were invented). Clothes make the man or woman.

Leave your shirt out. This will make you look longer from the neck down. If you do the opposite and tuck your shirt in, you will be accenting your waist. Many have skinny legs and shoulders and carry their weight in their middle. I am like that. It is called "shaped like a pear." If anyone tells you that you need to get in shape, tell them what I say. "I am in shape, a pear is a shape," and also a very nice fruit. Also, leaving your shirt out helps send a message that you are an approachable, easy-going person. Sometimes people with perfect shapes make me nervous.

Vertical stripes. Wear clothes with vertical stripes. Did you ever see a heavy sports referee or prisoner? No? Vertical stripes are the reasons. Most are overweight. Many families keep prison pictures in their photo albums. "Look at how thin your grandmother looked when she was in prison." Psychologists will tell you the following: "People's eyes follow the stripes from top to bottom and their brains say, "This is a lot of work following this; these people must be tall and thus—skinny."
In times of war, God forbid, or if you end up in a coma, again, God forbid, you will need that extra weight to survive. Skinny people cannot remain in a coma for a month. Some of my relatives could survive a half year. By then, the doctors should have figured out how to wake them up. Unless it is an HMO, then we need to give them an extra month.

Baggy clothes hide extra weight. No problem with that. Also, baggy clothes can hold more stuff in your pockets, like cell phones, keys, golf ball retrievers, and bike tire pumps. Thin people usually don't wear baggy clothes. Some of their pants are so tight they can't get a tube of chapstick into their pocket. If we can convince thin people to wear baggy clothes, then we will be indistinguishable and eat that Junior Whopper at Burger King. Which is kind of nice.

Be confident in your look; your body and others will follow. Most people of all sizes and shapes lack self-confidence.

Be confident in the way you look, and others will want to be around you. Maybe they or some relative might even pick up a dinner check once in a while.

I always remember my uncle Armen, who was harassed by his friends for being overweight. At eighty-five, he tipped the scales at, well, who cares. One friend asked him what his doctor thought about the excess weight. Uncle Armen took the sandwich out of her mouth, wiped his third chin, and said, "My doctor's dead."

Here is a joke that has absolutely nothing to do with the above. A recent study shows that people who laugh are less likely to have food in their mouths. Most psychologists and psychiatrists are overweight. See? I just made that up.

Speaking of psychiatrists, a man goes to his lawyer and says, "I think I am a moth." The lawyer says, "Why don't you go see your psychiatrist?" The man answers, "I would have, but your light was on!"

The Bible tells us, "We are fearfully and wonderfully made."

Garbo tells us, "No sadness—love yourself and others will also."

Reunion: Looking for Dad

My car leaves the driveway on a gray misting morning. It is the type of gray morning that brings out all the nagging problems of the day—whether the kids, the office, or some relationship that gnaws at you. It plays with your gut since your mind is not awake enough to calm things down. These feelings are magnified by the lack of sun.

Today, even the gray sky cannot stop my excitement. My thoughts reach past the now rhythmic movements of the windshield wipers beating away the rain that has started. I am heading to my first *USS The Sullivans* ship reunion in place of my dad. The year before he passed away, I wanted to take him to one of his ship's reunions, but he told me he wouldn't know anyone. This is from a guy who used to strike up conversations with strangers in elevators. That was four years ago. Now I am heading to Deerfield, Illinois, to find the Marriot Hotel where the World War II destroyer ship, the *USS The Sullivans,* reunion is taking place.

I have no clue where Deerfield, Illinois, is. I could have Googled it or used my phone for directions, or simply taken the time to print it. Like my father before me, who had time for that? Just drive.

Just drive. The gray begins to lighten, and I turn off the windshield wipers remembering an episode as a child when my father was driving in Chicago, and we were looking for a hotel. Sitting secure in the back seat, without seatbelts on, my young sister Patty and I stared up at the big skyscrapers. These were something we had never seen before. Dad stopped along a Chicago street, and my mother rolled down the window. Dad beckoned some stranger walking down the street, "Say, fella, how do I get to the Sanford Hotel?" The guy kept walking. My dad waited and then yelled the same thing to another guy who happened to get too close to the car window. This guy stopped, bent down, and began to give us sincere directions.

"Uh-huh, uh-huh," Dad said as the guy kept pointing and using his hands as if conducting a symphony. Slowly, Nazar took his foot off the brake and let the car drive away as the guy kept talking and pointing—unaware that he was no longer being listened to.

Mom snapped her head and said, "Nazar, the guy is giving you directions; you aren't even listening!"

The car was now twelve feet away, and the street guy was still talking while he hustled to keep up with the moving car.

"Aw, what the hell does he know?" Dad said as Patty, and I laughed and laughed.

I will be Nazar today.

Who needs instructions? It is just a hotel. It has a sign. It occupies space. It will be there, and I will find it.

Not wanting to talk to a stranger, I called my cousin Nancy.

"Hey, is Deerfield south of O'Hare?"

"Just a second," she said without missing a beat. Who knows what I had interrupted. I am rude. No "hello," just, "hey." Nancy is used to giving advice but rarely is there a question. She tells me all the things she has to do today and how some people were supposed to stay with them and then canceled at the last minute. It wouldn't have been so bad, but she spent the whole day cleaning the house and making "Get-A-Goor" (a massive Armenian buffet to feed eight people. Only two people were showing up!).

When you talk with an Armenian in our extended family, you get the story, but you also get commercials. I didn't want to hang up on her. I needed the info, but as long as the teller has the listener on the line, you will listen to what they think is important, then they will tell you the story, add a commercial, then more story.

"Stay on the tollway, and it is by Lake Forest; Saunders Road, take a right," Nancy concludes.

I take her instructions into my head. Twenty minutes later, I call my wife and tell her where I was.

"I am on the Edens Expressway near Skokie."

"You passed it. Turn around," she tells me. "Google it on your phone, and next time, print instructions."

Google it? What the hell does Google know?

I find it. I have a mental conversation as I march into the lobby. Don't get emotional. You are the kid of the sailor; you didn't fight the war. Don't ask stupid questions. For God's sake, don't start to heave your shoulders and cry.

I walk to the front door of the hotel and see an older woman followed by a man with a *USS The Sullivans* hat covering his white hair.

"Hi, my dad was on *The Sullivans* in 1943, I and am coming to the reunion," I blurt out to this perfect stranger.

"Nice to meet you. I served on the ship during the Korean War," he announces. "They are all meeting in room 739 inside."

The Korean War wasn't that long ago, was it? Those Korean War vets should look young, shouldn't they? I guess not. How old will the guys look who served with dad?

Finally, I walk into the room. I pick out the oldest-looking fellow and tell him my story. Sorry, served on the *USS The Sullivans* during the Korean War. Then another. Finally, two young fellows who served in the 1960s greet me. Richard Cuttone, Hal, his wife, Nancy, and others take me under their wing and begin to talk.

"You need to talk with Al," Rick exclaims. "He served with your father, and, to be honest, there are not that many left who are able to come to the event."

Coming across the room, a hunched-over sailor, gray hair peeking out below his proud *USS The Sullivans* hat, grabs a seat next to me.

"Here I am. What do you want to know?" he asks.

Art Schmitt, from Cairo, Illinois, served with my father.

I show him my dad's picture. Time takes its toll. Sadly, he did not remember him. Later I realized that I did not remember half the kids in my first-grade class. How would he remember one guy out of 300 from seventy years ago?

"Tell me some stories, Art," I ask.

With a sparkle in his eyes and a big grin on his tired face, he does. For two hours, he has my attention. He starts from the beginning. The five Sullivan brothers who enlisted in the navy asked to be put together on the same ship. Their reason: "We stick together." That became the motto for the ship named after them. There was an unbreakable bond of family, an unflinching conviction that five brothers together could serve their country in a greater measure than leading separate lives. The navy did not like the idea of these Waterloo, Iowa, boys serving on the same vessel but gave in to their wishes. They were to serve on the cruiser ship named *The Juneau*.

On a dark, moonless night, Japanese torpedo planes dropped their deadly cargo. The *Juneau* was hit by a torpedo. Dangerously listing and partially filled with water, the *Juneau*, along with other injured task-force ships, limped back to base. One of the Sullivan brothers was injured, and the other was below deck in the engine room when a second torpedo struck the ship about eight hours later. Apparently, according to Art, it hit in the same spot, which was right next to the ammunition, and lit various explosive gases. Like a volcano, the *Juneau* exploded, lifting itself out of the water, splitting in half, and sinking in forty-eight seconds.

The remaining ships in the task force were also damaged. The task force captain had to make a decision: stay and look for survivors or get the task force, with 2,000 sailors, out of the range of the new Jap torpedo attacks. With wounded ships and having seen the *Juneau* explode before his eyes, the fleet captain left for the safe repair base. When he arrived in protected waters, he put out a report to send search crafts to the area where the *Juneau* sank. The paperwork got shuffled and filed. Three days later, the paperwork was found.

There were 520 men who went down with the *Juneau* in those forty-eight seconds. However, 160 survived in the water, including one Sullivan brother. Planes flew over these men and radioed to send help. Those pilots filed papers also. Thinking that someone must be on their way, the radio signals to base were virtually ignored. Eventually, the papers and reports were found, and by the eighth day, by order of the admiral of the navy, a major rescue mission was set up to save the injured sailors of the *Juneau*.

Thirst, unbelievable injuries soaked in salt water, flaming oil burns, and frenzied shark feedings had taken their toll. The only remaining Sullivan brother, delirious, jumped overboard from the lifeboat, "needing to take a shower." Circling sharks ended his service. The rescue ships arrived shortly. Ten men were alive!

The final death toll was 687, including the now-famous five Sullivan brothers.

"The brothers' parents were notified of their deaths on January 12, 1943. That morning, the boys' father, Thomas, was preparing to go to work when three men in uniform—a lieutenant commander, a doctor and a chief petty officer—approached his front door.

"I have some news for you about your boys," the naval officer said. "Which one?" asked Thomas. "I'm sorry," the officer replied. "All five."

Art, like my dad, met the mom and dad of those Sullivan boys. In September of 1943, at the ship's commissioning dinner, a bunch of eighteen-year-olds shook the parents' hands. They were simple folk from the rich farmlands of Waterloo, Iowa, making the ultimate sacrifice. Five boys. Five boys who played baseball together, wrestled with each other and made a game of teasing their younger brothers.

During and after that dinner, Art and my dad, along with 300 men, got the "fire in their belly." The fire helped drive out the fear and homesickness. They got the honorary title of "Plank Owners." This means they were the first on the newly commissioned boat.

Art proudly displayed that tag on his hat.

"You looking for me?" Jack Holder says.

Jack served with Dad also.

"Your dad was a radar man? I knew all of them. I must have known your dad. I was on the deck when they started bombing Iwo Jima. I was four feet away from the five-inch guns when the force of the blast knocked me on my rear end. I couldn't get up as the gun kept sending shell after shell. By the time the twenty-fourth shell was fired, I was deaf in my right ear. Haven't heard a thing out of that ear for seventy years. I get $800 a year disability for that injury," Jack proudly exclaims.

"You should get $2,000 a year," I interrupt. "My dad said he ate candy bars for two years—no food, just candy bars on ship."

"The candy bars all had worms in them," Jack explains, "and when we rescued the pilots that crashed into the water, we got fifteen gallons of ice cream for returning the pilot. The captain and his staff got five gallons, the officers got five gallons, and 300 of us got five gallons. My take was a tablespoon of ice cream. That's it, a tablespoon! We saved the guy's life! And rotten candy bars. I don't know how your father survived on those candy bars. "

Tall Short Stories from the Comedic Mind of Garbo

Their stories continue—some my father told me, some he didn't.

"Your dad got written up for peeing overboard? Hell, we peed all the time overboard."

"We stripped the Jap prisoners we got and gave them shorts to wear; one of them had a $100 Hawaiian bill on him."

"Two men were picked up by a wave and fell overboard, and I jumped into the water and grabbed them both. They fed me a line, and we got them back on the ship."

"On one of the Pacific islands, there was a long, long line. The line snaked around until it came to a hut. Some native women were "entertaining" the men for $2 each."

"We ate baked beans and rice for breakfast. To this day, I won't touch the stuff."

"Our bunks were stacked three high—300 men."

"We bounced bullets off the water at low-flying kamikaze planes. One plane flew by, and we fired so many bullets into it, it just dissolved before our eyes; only the engine and propeller continued on for about 100 feet and then fell into the ocean."

"During the worst typhoon to hit the US Navy, *The Sullivans* was able to fill half of her oil tanks, the other half the captain filled with water. He had great wisdom. Another destroyer did the same. We were inches away from tipping over in the 180-mile-an-hour wind. Three other destroyers were not able to fill up on the oil and were being bounced around by the now-ninety-foot waves. We tried to get some sleep, and by the next morning, I went on deck, the three destroyers were gone."

This tremendous storm ended the lives of over 600 sailors on those destroyers.

"We pulled over a hundred men out of the water from the *Houston* and the *Bunker Hill*. Both were hit by kamikaze planes. Many were burned from the flaming oil floating on the water. If you jumped off the deck of an aircraft carrier, you could not survive. It was too high up. The captain tipped the aircraft carrier to get the spilled fuel off the flight deck and into the water. Along with the fuel, men were jumping off the aircraft carrier's deck to avoid the fires breaking out all over.

Chuck "Garbo" Hajinian

On *The Sullivans*, one guy, George Mendonsa, steered *The Sullivans* to get these boys out of the water. Being seven years old, when his family moved their fishing business from Portugal to the New Jersey coast, he knew how to steer a boat in all kinds of weather. His skill at moving *The Sullivans* saved many men. He later saw how these burned, and injured sailors were cared for by the nurses on the hospital ships. Being on leave in downtown Manhattan when the war with Japan ended, he went out to the streets to celebrate along with all of New York City. Overwhelmed with emotion, he grabbed a nurse, the kind of nurse that saved so many of his fellow sailors, and gave her a big kiss. A kiss so famous, a kiss that bent the girl back, right on the lips!! The war was over! A famous photographer, Alfred Eisenstaedt, captured five years of pent-up emotion. This picture first appeared inside *Life* magazine. Thirty years later, the famous picture made the cover of *Life* magazine. This was the first time George saw the picture, and he promptly sued *Life* for not being compensated as the subject for such a famous picture. He won. *Life* appealed, and his attorney told him he couldn't fight *Life*. George instead wrote a book. The woman he kissed was not his wife. She was in the background of the picture. The woman kissed was a dental assistant, not a nurse. George is still alive at ninety." George would die five years later at the age of ninety-five.

As a side note, on Thanksgiving 2014, at my dad's brother Garbo's home, I met a man named Bill who claimed to be the person who kissed the girl in the famous picture. Apparently, there were three or four who claimed to be the guy, and they were all on the *Larry King Live* talk show. Bill said the photographer said it was him forty years later.

The stories continue. That night, at the celebration dinner, I ask if I could address these men and their wives. The reunion chairman says that would be fine and hands me the microphone.

What is it about Armenians that they feel the need to talk? All the time? What makes what comes out of our mouths so important? We can't walk by a neighbor without looking for eye contact and saying hi. We start conversations with people in the grocery line. Twenty seconds in an elevator is too long not to talk about sports or the weather with a total stranger until his floor comes up. When there is no one in the elevator, I start to hum.

My mind asks me the same question as my sweaty hand grabs the mike. Before me are ninety men and women who were finished with dessert and were having table conversations. How do I interrupt? What right do I have to interrupt? Being embarrassed takes a back seat to saying something that is bursting inside. The words are not prepared.

"Hi, excuse me a moment. I must be the youngest guy here (*What kind of opening is that? Brilliant.*). Anyway, seventy years ago, my dad served on *The Sullivans* from 1943 to1945, and I want to thank all of you for letting me share in the first day of your reunion. I got a chance to meet some of you who served on the ship in the early 1960s, right in the middle of the Cuban Missile Crisis. I met those who fought in the Korean War on *The Sullivans*. Some of you spent time with the ship during peacetime. Three of you here tonight served with my dad in 1943. Somehow in God's plan, *The Sullivans* survived the worst typhoon while sadly other destroyers didn't. I hope your sons and daughters and their children can share in these reunions and to experience how much all of you have given to our country. My dad passed away three years ago. I came to find him in the stories and the faces of the men he served with. I can say tonight I have. Thank you for your stories and for welcoming me. God Bless all of you."

A number of veterans come up and shake my hand. I soon leave the hotel.

The highway winds around, the traffic is light. The setting sun brings wetness to the corner of my eye. Both proud and melancholy, I whisper, "Well, Dad, we made a reunion. Thanks, Pa."

Quarantine #4 We are made of Clay—Easter News

"Besides, I wanted to be an atheist but didn't care for their holidays. Either way, atheist or not, good health is the slowest way to die. We are all headed to simply stop moving—but the comic has a soul."

Garbo

Comedy, always comedy.

I still remember the scene in the movie *Blade Runner,* where this android warrior, Roy Batty (played by Rutger Hauer), meets his human creator and asks him to extend his life. The scientist responds that his model was designed to expire after a certain amount of time. Grabbing the scientist by the neck, Batty tries to explain why as he chokes his creator to death.

Batty: I've seen things you people wouldn't believe. Attack ships on fire off the shoulder of Orion. I watched C-beams glitter in the dark near the Tannhauser gate. All those moments will be lost in time ... like tears in rain ... Time to die. Quite an experience to live in fear, isn't it? That's what it is to be a slave.

There will be no extension of his life. The android, devoid of a soul, created by man, will simply stop moving.

I told an atheist one day, "Do you know when you cut yourself, there are over eleven chemical reactions that take place to stop the bleeding?" How is that possible without an intelligent designer? And why would He care if we stopped bleeding?

Long Short Drive to a Sub Sandwich

We spend our high school times wanting to be seen as worthy. Worthiness can sometimes come from having a pretty girl on your arm. You long for it. You search the mirror for reasons that might display a flaw. The mirror, without words, makes you happy or sad. At school, you become the mirror. You scan your friends and evaluate the faces of the girls that they have gone on dates with. You attempt dating. You fail. At seventeen, your dating life seems to be over. You gather much courage and try again. Then, when you are so low that you are playing handball with the street curb, you find someone. You have won your date's heart. She laughs at your jokes, she smiles. Her beauty takes days to fully understand and appreciate. You are standing tall. Others notice too. For that brief moment in your life timeline, you become the center of her universe. You can feel in your veins—now you are worthy, now you are somebody. The mirror is your friend. Your head has a constant, indescribable warmth. A magnificent bond has occurred between you and this siren. Those ever-revealing, shadowy eyes, that nose, those full pink lips. Then, somehow, it becomes hard for you to take a breath. In the rare bizarro universe, a switch has been clicked, and you are no longer interested. Fear and flight take over. The warmth, the reason, disappear. In the ever-growing emotional tornado going on in your body, you don't know why, but you want out.

Wanting to drop off this date, Tom Orion sat in the back seat while her chestnut-brown hair framed her big green eyes. She plays a major card and asks Tom if he would go to the turnaround dance. Wrong direction, he thinks. Tom starts making excuses as to why it would not be a good idea. Tom starts to feel sweat bead on his forehead and underarms. Driving was his best buddy, George. Two blocks to go, tears are forming in her eyes. Suddenly, he feels like a total jerk. He wants this ride to be over. Both are aware of the intense emotion, and time is not moving it forward. This is because his good buddy is slowing down the car from 25 to 10 miles an hour. His big grin and 1960s black framed glasses are clearly visible in the rearview mirror. This is George's car but Tom's movie. The rearview mirror reveals George is having the time of his life. Tom is squirming. His tense neck is twisting his head in a painful way.

"You are a great kid; there are lots of other guys that will go to the turnaround with you," he lamely explains. Her eyes close, tears fall unwiped. Where once there was romance; now, the pain of resignation fills the back vinyl seats. George struggles to hide his huge smile.

Finally, they make it to her home. Tom jumps out and takes her to the door. Her eyes never leave his. Her tears continue to drip; a goodbye hug and a rush back to the car. Tom throws himself into the back seat wanting to cover himself with an unseen blanket.

"Just bury me," he snarls.

His buddy, who has backed the car out of the driveway, starts laughing. "Hey, Casanova, how about a sub sandwich?"

"Sure," Tom says, covering his head with his sweater.

George peels out of the driveway. Subs heal.

Two Stories from the Moon

On a winter night in Michigan, I half woke to the dropped temperature in my bedroom. It was cold. Technology has used the internet to lower the furnace output, and my subconscious was ticked. I fought to stay in my swirling dream state. Grabbing my covers, ignoring intruding awareness, I refused to wake up. The fetal position remained. My cotton thoughts slowly slid back to the dream state of oblivion as my teeth were set, the covers wrapped, and sweet sleep re-embraced me.

Unaware of time, feeling wonderful in my ethereal state, an intruder pierced the darkness. From the skylight above, the moon slid directly in position to act like a mirror of the sun. It sent a direct spotlight to the corner of my eye. The white light caused havoc as my brain tried to grasp the source of the intrusion. The body fought to ignore it. Sleep is pleasure. Pleasure is good. Curled up, snuggling sleep is the best. The moon was having none of that. The light seemed to be pulsating and getting brighter as I opened my eye. It was the moon. I was now awake. The moon knows no boundaries. Its light has no discretion. It has no light of its own but reflects a greater light guided by a never changing millennial time schedule.

That is the moon's purpose.

It was supposed to be a secret. My girlfriend's parents were going out of town, and we were going to have about eight friends over to hang out. Word spread like a winning lottery number, and by 8 p.m. on Friday night, seventy high schoolers had plied their way into the house, and a major party was taking place. Some brought some beer.

Some had some unshared pot. Most just hung out with their hands in their pockets, making stinging comments to others who had their hands in their pockets. Girls covered parts of their mouths while their eyes darted from side to side. A few slipped upstairs to the bedrooms. Most walked around this huge suburban house, checking out what would never appear in their homes. Soon uninvited guests arrived.

BUSTED! The police, scores of them, came in the front door. Word quickly spread, and the original group of eight of us escaped out the back cellar door and ran, scattering into other yards. Unbelievable laughter came from all of us as we scampered like dogs jumping and tumbling over shrubs, fences, pots, and garden statues. What luck. The moon was out to guide our flight. Hiding behind some bushes, we saw the flashing red lights and the line of interloper party crashers being questioned by the officers of peace and quiet.

Some of the men in blue came around the backyard with flashlights. My scared girlfriend held me. The moon hid us with its brightly lit shadows. The police went back to the front. My buddies laughed as if someone was vigorously tickling them, and they held their breath not to laugh out loud.

"Great party, Aimee," I told my girlfriend. "Good thing you ordered the moon."

There is no color with the moonlight. It is simply black or white. This time, there was a hint of pale yellow.

Lifting her forehead, one of the prettiest foreheads in memory, she let it fly, "Moon or no moon, you are in real big trouble for not keeping this party a secret!"

The moon can be a harsh mistress.

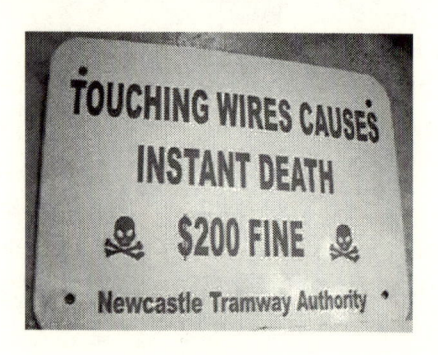

TOUCHING WIRES CAUSES INSTANT DEATH
☠ **$200 FINE** ☠
• Newcastle Tramway Authority •

Selling the Business

There he sat before me, hands wringing over and over as I signed the final documents. His business was now mine.

"Congratulations, you now own my business. You saw the numbers. I have poured my life into this business," said this man of many years.

He looked tired. Worn out. His forehead had unnatural wrinkles. His flesh lacked vibrancy. Sitting in front of his desk, I responded, "I have reviewed all these numbers, and it is quite impressive. You made a good living and have a good business formula for a man in his seventies."

His next response shocked me. Tears began to form in his eyes.

"I spent my whole life building this business. I worked six days a week, and on Sundays, I came in and did book work." After a long pause, he continued, "I never saw my children grow up."

The tears became sobs, heaving sobs. I had no words as he continued.

"You know, my wife told me so many times, we had plenty. I didn't listen to her pleadings. I always wanted a little more. Even after my second heart attack, I still wanted more. It was not a game but an obsession. I missed all the important things in my daughter's and son's lives. I refused to listen to my wife, my friends. She wanted to travel; now, she is so broken down, she can't walk to the corner. I did what I wanted to do. I thought I could trust my thoughts, my judgments. How wrong I was."

Pausing to wipe his eyes, he continued. "Listen to me. Don't believe everything you think. Don't be so damn stubborn. Listen to people."

Feeling like I had to speak to comfort this man, I said, "Well, now you can spend time with your grown children, and you won't have the stress of the business to think about."

"I so wish you see Chuck." He paused as he continued to wipe his eyes. "They have moved on with their lives. I was practically dead to them. Conversations revolved around the business and my accomplishments. Even on family vacations, I was on the phone. I was there but not really there. I thought I could justify things because I was making money. Everything was about the money and my damned ego to accumulate it. I am worth over $30 million, and you know what? I would give it all away to regain my youth and my health!"

I held my head down. The guy who always had a comeback, I was silent.

"Listen," he spoke, "enough of this; let's talk next week."

Finally sensing an end to the battle inside of him, I shook my head yes, gathered the closing documents, and began to leave as he softly revealed to me a final warning.

"Chuck, don't do what I have done."

I nodded and left.

In the Comfort of Someone's Living Room or "Sit Crooked, But Talk Straight"

> **AVOCADO: Hello I'm good fat**
>
> **BACON: *lights cigarette* *punches avocado***

Imagine a time with no cell phone, no television. Just a radio. Maybe three families out of ten had one. For entertainment, you had to look outside yourselves and ignore the constant neuronal feedback your brain is giving you about your comfort, your self-esteem, your fears, and your glance in the mirror.

You actually needed to be with someone face to face to know that you are okay and alive. You needed to look at their mouth move, to scan their face for blemishes, to catch the glimmer in their eyes. Especially if your English was rather poor. According to my dad, my Armenian grandfather loved to go to Charlie Chaplin movies. Here was the poor tramp, played by Chaplin to perfection. Through his wits, the tramp became successful: he got a free meal, won the girl of his dreams, and conquered the cold giant of a world before him. All without speaking English—or any other language. These were silent movies. Maybe a piano in the theatre played melodramatic music to accent the scenes. The piano player would be cued, and she (usually a woman—I just made that fact up—stay awake now) would play the same riffs during those dramatic scenes.

One evening, my Armenian grandparents found themselves in the living room of a good friend and distant relative. This was their television: Go to someone else's home and drink coffee, have some baklava dessert (fifty layers of fine rolled dough with crushed walnuts and a honey syrup baked and sectioned into diamond squares—three hours' work.), and talk. Talk about anything and everything. These living rooms were (air quotes) "maybe 12x13 feet" in size. Big, repeating flowered wallpaper adorned the already small room with a heat radiator with a metal cover against the wall. Also, like a badge of honor, a picture of the first family member to be married in America

So, three couples are enjoying themselves on a cool evening in September when the newlywed daughter comes in crying and sobbing about her new husband to her parents—oblivious to the two other couples. It doesn't really matter. They are not true strangers as all came from the same town of Tomarza in ancient Armenia, now Turkey—a town of about 10,000 Armenians who intermarried for close to 900 years! Village logic: "Why go to all that traveling to another village; look right here in Tomarza. How about the shoemaker's daughter? Not the prettiest, but you will never have to worry about shoes. They all put on weight later anyway!" We call that "friends with benefits" today, only they had to get married for the free shoes back then.

Everyone is a third cousin or a fifth great-uncle. Never written down, they verbally record it. This, of course, is sad because when Pa dies, we would ask, "Was this Bedros guy a third or fourth cousin to Auntie Siranoush?"

The response would be, "We didn't write it down; he is a relative on your ma's side." Jeez, no one had paper or pencil? Maybe my grandkids will need this information for a school project. What is he or she going to say? "My ancestors couldn't afford a pencil and knew nothing about paper."

Either way, having relatives is a badge of honor. It is their lifeline in the earthquake cracks of life that show up. Maybe fifty-sixty "close" relatives. This is a very important point for what comes next.

Few people today would ever comment, correct, or advise a stranger. Even at work, an employee must be given four compliments before a correction to their behavior is brought up. Hold your breath—a lawsuit coming? Sadly, today's families are not much better. A "helpful" correction of a sister-in-law's toddler or a cousin's manners, or a sibling's mean comedic comment can severe a relationship for years. How did we get so destructively self-righteous?

There is an Armenian saying that roughly translates into, "Sit crooked but talk straight." My aunt, who lived to be ninety-seven years old, would tell us this all the time, even when we were watching a Packer game. "Never mind touchdown!' Sit crooked and talk straight!." To this day, I don't know what the hell that means or why it was mentioned at such odd times. If you sit crooked, won't your back spasm? And talk straight—whose modern truth? Based on the behavior of my relatives, it could mean speaking the truth even though you are not perfect. People who live in glass houses can still throw stones if they can lift them, and they don't cost too much. Observed bad behavior needs to be corrected before some nonrelative, outcast stranger (called an ODAR) notices it and brings shame to our extended family. If there is a fire and you know where a hose is, it is your obligation as a member of the human race, for God's sake, to speak up! That's the Hajinian genetic logic and "gift." Hajinians determine which fire needs putting out. Okay, back to the story.

This young bride, with tears streaming down her cheeks, is being comforted by her mother. My grandfather, an unusually quiet and small-statured man, stands up and declares to the seven people in the room, including himself, that the real problem is the mother of the bride! She created this mess by her interfering in their marriage! What she said/did made the groom … the bride … come to this. How my grandfather knew this, no one knows. The speech lasts about thirty-five seconds. Seems like an hour to my grandmother. From a silent movie, Charlie Chaplin has spoken!

Well, we grown-up Hajinians, who were mere children when he would pass, if we were there, we'd say, "Yeah, Grandpa!" His wife, my grandmother, is mortified by his outburst. She sets down her coffee cup, stands up, and says, in her best formal Armenian, "Well, it's getting late; we should be going." So ended the story as told to me.

Two things were added to the story by the relatives: Meddling is important when young people are married—for the first year through the twenty-two years of marriage, but the girl's mother was too much of a meddler. Who determines how much meddling is appropriate? No one really knows. Like adding salt to a meal, you add until someone complains. And this was a very distant cousin of grandpa. So, it was okay what he said.

Soccer Number Eight in Armenia

Little eight-year-old Krikor Antramian wore the number eight on his jersey. His grandmother picked that number. It is a sacred number for Armenians. Churches are adorned with the eight-pointed star. It is the connection of eternity, somewhere out there, to life here. Krikor, at that early age, was a soccer phenomenon. His feet skills were noticed by the older coaches, and he played on teams two years older. By the age of ten, his number-eight jersey was followed by the Armenian national team as a future star. Even though he retired, his father was already one.

Krikor's family was from Artsakh, an ancient Armenian land that contained many churches and even the foundations of an ancient castle built around 70 BC by the famous Armenian king Tigrane "Medz" The Great. Around 1923, Joseph Stalin gave this mountainous enclave to a newly created country, Azerbaijan. When the Soviet Union broke up, this tiny enclave declared its independence. A war was fought from 1991-94 between these far-outnumbered mountainous Armenians and the massive oil-funded Azeri army. Throughout its history, Armenians have never started a war. They have always been invaded, and most of the time, they lost the battles. For some heavenly reason, all over the world, they survive as a people to this day. This time, they defeated a superior army and lived peacefully in their ancient Artsakh homeland, separated by mountains, from Greater Armenia.

Peace is but a fleeting moment prior to the next war. The next war came to Artsakh, and the families were again called to fight. Krikor's father, Ara, became a platoon leader not far from the village they lived in. Krikor, Ara, and Krikor's grandmother Catherine all lived in a small stone home on the sides of the mountain village. Krikor never knew his mother. She did not survive his birth.

Ara Antramian, an Armenian national soccer team star, would meet a similar fate to the 5,000 other soldiers from Artsakh when he was killed by an Azeri drone attack while he was defending his village. Unless a soldier is known personally, it is hard to grasp the violent death of this cancer called war. This death had a side story that could not be pushed aside. The morning of the drone attack, Krikor was running food to his father and his fellow soldiers when the missile that took his father's life tore into his tender left leg. He was immediately sent to the main hospital in Yerevan, the capital of Armenia. There, talented surgeons repaired what they could. He would then spend his next six months living in the Artsakh orphanage to rehab his damaged leg. His ability to run and cut quickly was gone. So was this gentle giant's soccer career. It made the news. Not just any news, but the national news. Unbeknownst to Krikor, he had become a symbol of survival. Number eight.

Grandma Catherine was a short, stocky Armenian grandmother. Her head was full of white hair. Her face could not conceal the many tragedies she had experienced in her life. She had also learned how to rise above and conquer. She would say, in a quote from the famous Armenian author William Saroyan, "I don't need happiness to be happy!"

Krikor needed a lift. This twelve-year-old had grown up much too fast and had seen too much. Krikor needed a dog, she thought. After talking to the orphanage, it was decided that all the kids there could use a mascot.

Grandma Catherine bought a dog. Not just any dog, but a Gampr puppy named Oscar. The Gampr is the national dog of Armenia. With a coat made up of any color, it always has a soft undercoat with short or long hair. They grow to be very large, achieving 130 pounds—the size of a large bull mastiff. Some of the small orphans would hug and ride Oscar.

Tall Short Stories from the Comedic Mind of Garbo

The leaves fell early as the brilliant summer sun began to calm down and the shadows became gentler. It was time for the city soccer championship for fourteen-year-olds. This was a major event in the city of Yerevan. Families would so look forward to seeing their relatives, neighbors, and friends at the stadium.

This Saturday, there was a massive crowd of over 6,000 people in this park-like stadium called Yerevan Orbita. Twenty teams have battled down to two. The Yerevan team called "Urartu" battled against the Artsakh team known as the "Nagorno-Artsakh."

"Hurry up, Krikor." Grandma Catherine had a plan. She knew with the damaged leg, each step was painstakingly slow, but his big smile said it all. "Wear your soccer shorts and shoes to show your support. I have Oscar on the leash."

Krikor, though puzzled by her request, followed her instructions.

"You can't bring the dog into this taxi," the driver admonished Grandma Catherine.

"My dear son, have you not heard of Krikor and Ara Antramian, the soccer stars of Armenia? Are you going to deny his dog a chance to see this game? Here, take some of these zilook bread sticks for your wife; she will be very thankful." Grandma Catherine opened her purse and grabbed a bag of zilooks as she forcefully pushed Oscar into the taxi.

"Well, I am not married," announced the taxi driver.

"We can take care of that another time; I have a niece in Artsakh," Grandma Catherine responded as Oscar licked the side of the driver's head.

Taking the long taxi ride, Grandma Catherine went into the stadium but took a shortcut to the field. Krikor followed behind her.

There before them was the gleaming green grass on a perfect sunlit Saturday. What a wonderful arena.

Running ahead of Krikor, who held Oscar. "Who is the coach here," Grandma Catherine bellowed.

"I am," A short, bald named Levon came forth.

Grandma Catherine took his hand and kissed it. Then she pulled something special out of her purse: the number-eight jersey. It was her son-in-law's number, and now it belonged to her wounded grandson. She told the story of soon-to-arrive Krikor, about his love of the game and how, while assisting his father's platoon, his leg was damaged so severely, he was unable to play. She spoke of the loss of his parents and finally asked, "Could this boy play in this game with his fellow teammates?"

"Medz Mideek, great-grandmother Catherine, this whole stadium knows the story of Krikor, his father, and the tragedy. This is the city championship game!" The coach exclaimed. "I know of what he could do in the past; I am truly sorry for all the bad things that have happened. There are many families here whose sons have worked for years to get to this tournament."

Then, pausing after looking at the crowd, he said, "Take him to the bench; I will not promise he will play."

Grandma shouted, "Hurry, Krikor; go to the bench. You are on the team," turning her head so Krikor could not see her tears. Oscar whined and shuffled his fist-sized feet. He was ready too.

"But Grandma. I don't have my uniform," Krikor protested.

Slowly opening her purse, she pulled out the famous jersey, the complete number, the Number eight. Removing his shirt, he put on the jersey for the first time in over eight months. Unknowingly, he was putting on a prophet's mantle.

Soon Krikor was greeted by his old teammates. Having him in uniform caused astonishment for some parents. They knew the story of Krikor, his sacrifice, and that of his family. For those who did not, word began to spread through the crowd. "The number eight, that is Ara Antramian's son." Even the opposing team was told about Krikor's presence on the bench.

In the final period, the game was tied 4-4. There were only forty-five seconds left. Some felt a good defense should be in place to wind down the clock and go into a game-ending shootout. The Urartu team had gotten to this championship game by winning two shootout games. They had tremendous fourteen-year-old forwards. Suddenly, a Nagorno-Arsakh player was tripped, and he was not getting up. The other players helped him off.

Coach Levon looked at the parents in the stands, then at his team. Finally, deep in thought, he looked at the ground, looked up, and nodded. The injured boy on the Nagorno-Artsakh team limped off the field.

The coach came up to Krikor and got on one knee. "This is for you, this is for your father, this is for all those who hold the dream of freedom in their heart. Krikor, you go in as a forward and score."

Turning his head away, Coach Levon ran his open hands over his closed eyes and through his hair. His assistant coaches watched in disbelief as the disabled Krikor was assisted onto the field by his former teammates.

Like a lit fuse, the people in the stands suddenly noticed the number eight on the jersey.

Their coach on the other team recognized the number. He had played with Krikor's father. He knew the story. During this timeout, the Urartu team huddled. His hands went up and down as he advised his young players what to do.

The parents in the stands began to stand up, some confused, some understanding. Krikor himself was the most surprised. His old teammates and the large crowd began to say his name slowly and quietly, "Krikor, Krikor, Krikor!!"

Oscar began to pull on the leash. Grandma Katherine struggled with all her frail strength to hold him back.

With the biggest grin his contorted face had ever shown, Krikor swayed one leg after another until the ball was passed to him. By this time, the forwards on the other team came up, and Krikor passed to a teammate. The ball could have been easily intercepted by the defensive fielders. But for some reason, they let the ball pass. Krikor's teammate passed the ball back to Krikor, who continued to use his damaged legs to move the ball forward. Finally, two midfielders who could have easily stripped the ball from him—well, they stood in place, almost at attention as an honor guard would. Krikor passed them and looked to pass to his old teammate, Hratch. He caught Krikor's eye and shook his head "no." The defenders spread like the Red Sea before Moses.

The people in the stands suddenly grew silent. A strong breeze began to come from the east. Family, friends, and neighbors watched in anticipation of something special.

Instinct took over, and the scar tissues of his young mind and heart were torn asunder. Krikor took the shot and, with his good leg, he kicked the ball toward the goal with all of his being. The force of that twist of his wounded leg caused him to fall directly onto his face. What happened next, he never saw. The ball bounced off the goalie's hand and into the net. The people already on their feet did something few do: they began clapping and cheering despite their team losing. Pandemonium of relief broke out. Even the losing team rushed around Krikor and lifted him up. Many people were weeping. This was a release of emotion beyond a fourteen-year-old's Regional Soccer Championship game. This was a people's release of a war lost—of 5,000 families without fathers, sons, and brothers. This was a healing that the nation needed.

Tugging on the leash held by Grandma Catherine, Oscar finally got free and chased after the ball.

"Krikor, Krikor, Krikor!" the fans began to shout, all now standing, many with tears in their eyes.

The team and their fans found a new hero that day. Even hunched over, white-haired Grandma Catherine rushed and kissed all the boys, saving her tears and a big hug for Krikor. Oscar whined and jumped until she petted his big head. Despite threats from Grandma Catherine and bribing of treats, Oscar would not release the ball.

There are two pictures on the wall at the Artsakh orphanage. One proudly displays a picture of Grandma, Krikor, and his Nagorno-Artsakh teammates next to the actual regional soccer trophy. In the other photo sits a very large Gampr named Oscar, holding the ball.

Treasure—The Island House on Nagawicka Lake

Mansion on Nagawicka Lake, 1893-1955

"Grandpa, can we go to the island house and explore?" A fastball down the middle, and I hit it. "Okay."

"YES!" Steven yelled to his seven-year-old brother, Nazar, and five-year-old cousin, Daniel, as he jumped up and down. Daniel had a full head of black hair, while his cousins had short-haired summer haircuts.

In case they didn't hear, he repeated it loudly. "GRANDPA IS TAKING US TO THE ISLAND HOUSE TO LOOK FOR TREASURE!"

Long before these grandchildren were born, I had a historical fascination with a mansion built in 1893 in the middle of a glacier-created lake in southeastern Wisconsin. Who would take the time to build out in the middle of a lake at that time? What wife would put up with this? You needed a rowboat to get to the island as power boats were nonexistent at this time. This was no simple lake cottage. It was four stories. There was no electric power. Fresh water came from a hand pump or windmill on the property. Large granite stones made up the foundation, and an old timer in his nineties told me that his father actually had hauled these stones by horse and cart over the frozen lake.

Lakes freeze in Wisconsin. You can walk on them. Ice fishermen drill holes in it and set up tents to catch hungry fish like northerns and walleye. Before the emergence of radio and long before television, three thousand people in the 1920s would stand on the frozen lake and watch horses equipped with special gripping horseshoes as they pulled race carts in a large oval around this majestic home. Before all of this, horses and carts hauled tons of granite rock from shore to island.

Getting on the Jet Ski, I carefully balanced the four of us as we made our way to the island house on Nagawicka Lake, or "Sandy Bottom" Lake, which was named by the Indians who lived along its shores. The four of us were ready to take off. This half-mile ride was not without its risks, as big boat waves would rock the Jet Ski left and right. I was worried. I am old. They thought this was a great adventure and laughed when we almost tipped in the middle of the lake. They are young. I nervously approached the pebble and sand water landing area.

"Grandpa, we can jump off the jet ski and swim to shore?" shouts Nazar as I pull to within ten feet of landing. Before I can answer, they are in the water.

Within seconds, they are on the shore yelling, "Come on, Grandpa. Let's go."

Steven imitates my favorite saying to people who move slowly, "Come on, Grandpa. "Chop chop! Ha ha!"

The four-story stone home was built by Samuel Howard. Samuel was an attorney in Milwaukee who, at Christmastime, filled the Milwaukee opera houses with toys and gifts. Then he invited all the orphanages to bring their children for great Christmas parties. No one knew he had paid for these things until his funeral in 1900 when it was revealed by the owner of the Schlitz Brewery during a moving eulogy. After his death, the home was taken over by four bachelors who used it as a hunting lodge. Note: it is a two-acre island in the middle of the lake, and there are no huntable animals. They played a lot of cards and apparently drank. Their one rule was if one of them died or married, which they considered equal, their 25 percent share of the home would go to the others. The last surviving bachelor would pass away in the late 1940s. Eventually, St. John's Military Academy bought the island and inherited the home. They used all of it for camping and military training. The walking paths they developed and used, we were about to discover.

There before us was a worn dirt pathway leading to various parts of this relatively small island. Branches brushed against my face as the boys ran ahead, pushing aside the small bush leaves that had invaded the path. The filtered "end of summer" sunlight lit their faces and their light brown and black hair as they turned around and smiled. Now twelve feet behind, I pause. I realize that they are my future. My time is passed. They will be the ones to carry on the Hajinian baton of dreams and accomplishments. I wish I could explain that to them. Filtered sunlight does that to the emotions.

The island house was quite amazing when it was built before electricity, telephones, and power tools. It had a windmill for pumping water and a wood-burning boiler to heat the house. On the upper floor, there was a ballroom. By 1955, the four-story home was in ruins, frequented by teenagers for purposes that teenagers do and vandals—I think the kind that invaded Rome in the 600s. St. John's Military Academy had had enough. The staircase to the second-story ballroom was collapsing. The Delafield Fire Department was called to burn it down. Country people laughed and said the DFD motto was, "We never lost a foundation." Only the hand-cut speckled granite, red, gray, and black, cream-colored bricks from Milwaukee and St. Louis, and the large metal boiler, now crushed, survive. Each one of those granite blocks was perfectly shaped and took a long time to carve and hand cut. These are mini works of art in themselves. They are now randomly buried, separated, and hidden at times by brush, trees, and dirt. We are about to come upon these newspapers of house history.

"Hey, I found a brick," yells five-year-old Daniel. Running over to see the brick, they each examine it as if it were a new Lego toy.

"Come over, you guys; look at these rocks. This is what made up the house," I point out.

Examining the large-cut granite foundation stones, the youngest, Daniel, asks, "What happened to the roof and walls, Grandpa?"

They were burned to the ground almost seventy years ago.

Pointing out the obvious, I continue, "These trees growing up in the middle of these rocks were not here when the house was built."

No one is listening to Grandpa and his obsession with history. There is treasure to be found. After five minutes, the attention and excitement of piles of carved granite rocks fade, and the boys take off down another path. Daniel says there is a cornfield on the island. Nazar says no, there isn't. Daniel gets weepy. I watch their little arms pump the air as they run.

Twenty-five years ago, some other little kids also explored this area with me. The sunlight lit their excited faces too. They were the moms of these boys, and they were my daughters. Who stole that time? Where did it go? My thoughts drift back. Little girls picking a flower, brushing the hair off their faces while they looked at the mansion from the picture I carried, now a ruined home. They tried to make sense of it. Now they are married and have their own households and kids to raise, nurture, watch, and be a part of their growing up. I can't recall each day, but the island house tells me I was here with them—and now with their children, my three grandsons. In the melancholy, there is a satisfaction of a second chance.

"Grandpa, you have to come now. Nazar found a piece of burnt wood, and (pausing to catch his breath) it has a nail in it!" Steven announces.

"Yes, it is a real nail, Grandpa. Do you think there is treasure nearby?" Steven asks.

"Oh wait, I saw this show where they found a wooden box, and it had all kinds of money and stuff!" Nazar explains.

"Gold?" Daniel asks.

"I think so. Yeah, gold and some kind of jewelry. Pirates!" Steven shouts.

"There are no pirates here," Daniel rebukes.

"There could be," Steven emphatically replies

Daniel rolls his eyes and laughs at Steven.

"You said Spiderman," Steven announces

"No, I didn't," Daniel explains. "I like Spiderman, but he is not here now."

"Come on, Grandpa; you have to see this," Nazar gently explains while his eyes sense I am mentally elsewhere.

"Okay, let's see that nail. Sure enough, it is from the island house in this picture," I say as I thrust my chest forward. "We found a piece of treasure over a hundred years old."

Nazar the skeptic challenges, "Okay, Grandpa. How do you know that it is a hundred years old? Maybe someone built something and left this here."

"See the head on the nail? It is square, which means it was cast. Cast nails were used in the 1800s."

Ignoring the evidence, Nazar disagrees, "I don't think it is that old."

Steven and Daniel are now distracted and begin a Spiderman debate as they run down the path toward the Jet Ski.

"Wow, wait for me!" I exclaimed. I thought, Wait for your Grandpa. I will always be a few steps behind you, watching you run, but I am always ahead of you, watching your way.

"I Am Right, You Are Wrong'"

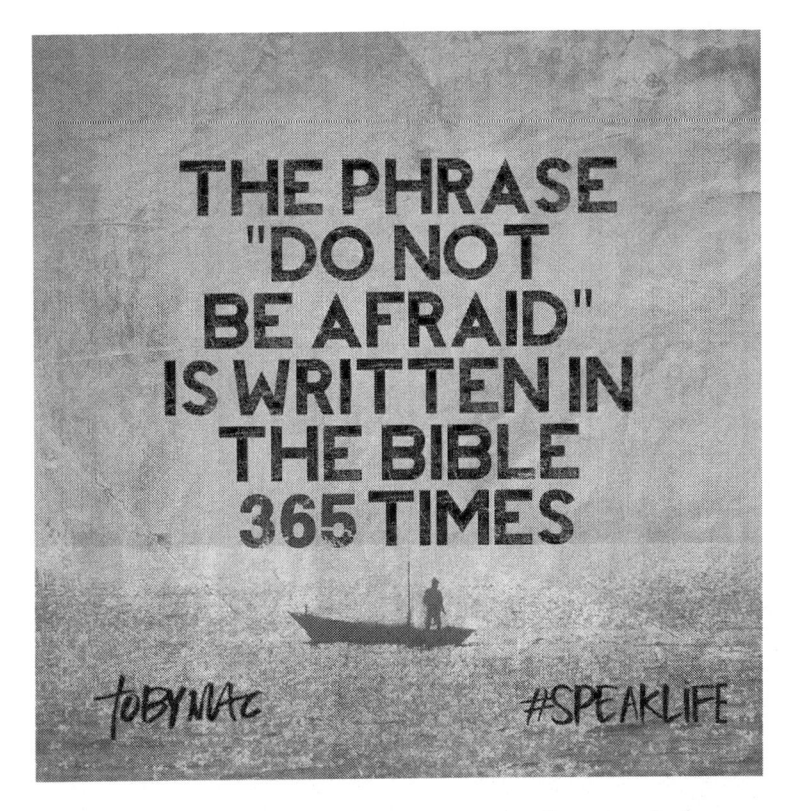

Disclaimer #1: This story is meant for entertainment. It is not meant to target or offend certain members of certain political parties, various religious or nonreligious people, scientists, historical persons, both living and dead, parents, grandparents, your relatives, my relatives, people who shop at Costco, vocalists, or other short story writers and also mathematicians. But, as they say, if the shoe fits, wear it, especially if it is a designer shoe with a soft leather insole. (My father was in the leather business).

Disclaimer # 2: I believe in absolutes. The battery that runs me is charged by absolutes (not Absolute vodka). One guy said he doesn't believe in absolutes. I replied, "Are you absolutely sure?"

Enough disclaimers already. Stop clenching your teeth. Here you go:

There are two groups of people (Yes, I know there are more than two, but do you want to hear the story or be right?): Group 1 and Group 2.

Group 1: I think there is a special room in heaven for Group 1, those who are always right. They get bunched together. "I am right, but enough of me telling you why. How about you tell me why I am right?" They have articles, videos, and the highest of highest special-intellect people that they listen to. You cannot get access to this portal of information easily. They like to point with their finger. There is power in pointing a finger. Try it sometime.

In their mind, they cannot hold two conflicting thoughts. They just can't. "The room is full. We cannot, will not, no sorry, our thoughts are packed like sardines." There is no doubt, no grey, no reflection. No real need to. In fact, physiological studies have shown that the fight-or-flight mechanism kicks in when they are contradicted. Adrenaline is released, which can be painful or make you feel very uncomfortable—"Can someone open a window in this bar?" I didn't research that, you know, with a double-blind test with a placebo. Someone in an elevator ride told me that, so it is probably true. I didn't ask why he was telling me. I got off on the next floor and walked the twelve floors up.

I love these Group 1 people. I really do. They are entertaining, and sometimes I have to put my hand up to my mouth to hide my giggling. It is like coming up behind someone and tickling them and getting a surprise jolt or innocent laugh. Okay, you'd better know them if you do that. To be honest, sometimes their words keep me awake at night.

"Maybe I should spend less time posting thumbs-up on Facebook and find out what I don't really know," as I sit eating potato chips. I do respect these people. They make the world interesting and truly get things done by acting on their convictions. As long as the stock market goes up, what harm can there be?

Group 2: They get to hang out in the fun parts of heaven. Can you imagine that? They don't have all the answers for one reason—they are men and women, not gods. They were never created to have all the answers, and to be correct in word, thought, and deed. Otherwise, we would see them as angels. No, there is something special in realizing that you and I might be wrong. It is freeing. I no longer have to be a god. I can still be a godly person. I personally like to throw my pillow on their couch and hang out until they say, "Hey, Chuck. The movie ended about an hour ago. We are going to bed; maybe you could let yourself out?"

They make up their own statistics: "Four out of three people have trouble with fractions!" Who can argue with that?

The following quote was attributed to Saint Francis of Assisi. Lots of beautiful, lifesaving quotes are attributed to him. Some he never said. In fact, if all the quotes attributed to SFoA were correct, the Saint would have never had time to eat.

"Come on, Francis, join us for dinner!" shouts his fellow monks. His reply could have been, "Hey, can't you guys see that I am talking and sharing wisdom for future generations? No time for food!" Eyewitnesses said he was a slim guy—so who knows?

Enough speculation. Here is what he said. It is so simple, and that is what makes it brilliant:

"It is better to understand than to be understood."

Disclaimer #3: The following is an example. It is a comedic attempt to explain. I use Baptists as a vehicle. It could be any group (especially those of the political Whig Party; they really screwed things up for America in the 1840s. Can I get an amen?). I love and respect Baptists. My son-in-law serves as a head pastor in a Baptist church. Most will understand, especially in Group 2. I did not originate this joke, and I know it is funny because I have heard other comedians tell it.

This story takes place in San Francisco on the famous Golden Gate bridge.

There was a fellow named Sam who was on the Golden Gate Bridge. Sam was down on his luck and was about to let go of the rail and fall to his death when another person came out of their car and ran to the man and shouted, "Don't let go! Do you believe in God?"

Sam replied, "Yes," as he looked down, his feet swinging over the water.

The other man, wiping his forehead, said, "Good, good. You have so much to live for. Are you Catholic or Protestant?"

Sam replied, "Protestant," as his hands clung to the bar above his head.

"Good, good. I am here to help. Lutheran or Baptist?"

Sam replied, "Baptist."

The helper was ecstatic, "Beautiful answer, wonderful, please don't let go. Southern Baptist or Northern Baptist?"

Sam replied, "Northern Baptist," as his fingers began slipping and his feet began to swing freely below his stretched body.

The helper reaching down to grab his hand, asked one last question, "Good, so good! Are you Northern Baptist, 1891 Convention or Northern Baptist, 1910 Convention?"

Sam, running out of strength, whispered, "1891 Northern Baptist Convention."

The helper pulls his hands back and yells, "Die, heretic!"

How life imitates comedy. Never, ever lose your compassion for those who do not think like you. From the '60s, I learned that compassion is not conditional. No, I did not wear beads.

A paraphrase from Matthew the tax collector's Gospel: "And while His disciples were debating who was the greatest amongst them, Jesus brought a little child into their midst and said, "Unless you become like this little child, you will never enter the Kingdom of

Heaven; whoever humbles himself like this little child is the greatest in the Kingdom of Heaven."

I am wrong, you are wrong. Let's go play.

The Ageless Phillip Dugas of New Orleans

A few blocks off the busy party streets of New Orleans sits a row of homes. Like any street in the middle-class America of the 1980s, it has a side driveway and a small porch. Most homes and neighborhoods are quite nondescript. This one was no exception. No, not really true. This home at one time housed the direct relatives and descendants of a drawer and painter of ballerinas, women bathing, and horses. He was the French impressionist Edgar Degas. In fact, you can tour his relatives' home and see the bedroom in which Degas slept back in 1873. A year later, he returned to France and with other French artists who would invent the French Impressionist movement.

That was then; this is now. It seems that the neighbor boys realized that a very old man lived in one of the houses right next to the Degas home. Some even said that this old man was a distant Degas cousin. His name was Philip Dugas. His window shades were always drawn. He rarely came out and had his food delivered at first by a young woman. I say at first because she seemed to get older as time went on.

Johnny Columbo was a couple of years older than us, in our early teens. He was one of the cool kids. He smoked cigarettes and liked to say, "Go tell your mom she wants you home," which made little sense to me. Johnny Columbo also liked to swear.

"You dumbass," he would sneer when we would drop the football during a neighborhood game on the lot next to the house next to the Dugas house.

Odd things began to take place in the neighborhood, or at least I began to notice. It seemed that Johnny Columbo was wearing nicer clothes, and he got himself a real nice car—a brand-new 1980 Corvette. He had a more mature look to him. Like he was no longer a teenager and was now in his twenties.

"Hey, Johnny. You don't have a job. Where you gettin' the money to buy a car like that?" asked my buddy Tony.

"None of your damn business, you useless turd!" Johnny shot back after lighting a cigarette.

Then one day, the police showed up at Mr. Dugas's house. Apparently, the lady who had been bringing him his groceries, well, she died on his porch. This was quite a scene. She had collapsed on the steps to the porch and was just lying there wearing a skirt with an apron and a white blouse. She looked like she was old and feeble. Her once-black hair was as white as the New Orleans clouds. The police questioned Mr. Dugas on his porch. This was quite a spectacle as parents and children alike stood around on the street in a semicircle to watch the interrogation of this man whom they rarely had seen. He was a hidden celebrity, a neighborhood legend, a ghoulish story man from yesteryears.

"He used to own three of the bars on Bourbon Street in the 1890s through the 1940s. My parents knew of him," remarked Mrs. Columbo, Johnny's mom.

"Yes, he owned the Red Head bar right across from Antoine's. He became one of the richest men on Bourbon Street in New Orleans. No wife, no kids, but plenty of women chased this guy," divulged another bystander.

"Rumor has it his mother's family was from a bunch of Creole doctors out in the boundary waters just outside of New Orleans," volunteered another spectator.

"How did they know these things, and why didn't I ever hear of this? How could he have run a bar business from 1890 through the 1940s and still be alive today?" I asked some of the adults.

"Never you mind. You kids, just stay the hell away from him and that house. I worry about you even playing in that lot next door," remarked my mom.

Soon the police finished their investigation, and the body was led away on a stretcher. As the attendants began to put the fully covered dead body into the back of the ambulance, her arm fell out over the stretcher. All of us jumped because the arm was so shriveled up—like it had been in the grave already.

"Who was that lady?" I asked

"Nurse Rambert, Rose Rambert," replied a woman in the group.

"Why, she went to school with my sister; my sister is fifty-one years old. She looked like she was 100," mumbled our neighbor's mom.

The ambulance left, lights flashing, and we all went our separate ways.

The years passed, and our yard football games were replaced by cars. We never had cars like Johnny. He traded in his corvette for a Mercedes. He also looked older. His hair began to gray.

I left New Orleans to go off to college. My family would follow and leave the old neighborhood. I continued on to graduate school with a new wife and a new career, but a chance business convention brought me back to New Orleans. The streets were as alive as I remember them back in my youth. The Dueling Piano Bar, dinner at Antoine's, the cabarets—it never changes. The only difference was the women. I noticed them now—those with overflowing bosoms and painted eyes, the bars, the music, the muffuletta sandwiches.

By chance, I decided to visit the old neighborhood and see who was left. All of my friends had left for opportunities in big cities. Most of their parents had died or moved away. However, one familiar face, though aged, still remained. Mrs. Columbo, Johnny's mom, sat on the porch rocking back and forth.

"Mrs. Columbo, it is me, Ted McNamara!" I waved and shouted.

"Oh, Teddy. Is that really you? I can't believe it. No longer the teenager, you have become a young man."

"Don't get up, ma'am," I said as I bounded up the steps and gave her a brief hug.

"Please pull up a chair," she ordered as she rocked back in forth in the spring morning sunshine.

From that point on, she would talk for over an hour, reporting on every incident that took place in my absence. So and so became a doctor, this girl became a mother of eight, and the twins opened a restaurant in New York City. The next thing she said, well, I just could not believe: Her son Johnny was dead. He died at the age of thirty-two. But he looked like a ninety-year-old, she explained. What she said next was beyond belief. The New Orleans atmosphere is known for its history and its mysterious past. But this time, this story, on a warm shadow-filled sun-lit porch with the spring heat, well, it changed me forever.

"Would you like some iced tea? I have a pitcher right here and an extra glass," she offered.

"Why, yes, thank you, Mrs. Columbo," my parched throat thankfully replied.

"Call me Agnes. You are a grown man now, Teddy," she announced as she poured a glass.

"Agnes, what happened to Tony after I left?" I eagerly asked.

Agnes would begin to tell me how the neighbor teenagers and young adults would be doing things for Phillip Dugas and how strange things began to happen. They would begin to age. Their skin would develop wrinkles. Some would lose their hair. But before that happened, their hair would turn gray.

"My son Johnny, your football buddy, well, he spent time over at Dugas's house. He started buying all kinds of things. No one knew where he got the money, and one day he just died," recalled Agnes while she pointed a finger at me.

"I don't understand," I quizzed.

She would continue to tell how Phillip Dugas knew all the politicians, how in the 1920s, he knew where the nuns buried the bodies of the babies they conceived. He knew all of the owners of the showplaces and entertainment areas, the real owners, not the fronts who actually are on the premises.

"That's impossible. My grandparents were teenagers in the '20s and they died long ago. How could Phillip Dugas own bars in the 1890s and still be alive in the 1980s?

Agnes would reveal the secret: he traded his money for time. Phillip Dugas, through his Creole ancestry and their mystery potions, somehow had the ability to take someone's youth and add it to his. She spoke about how the doctors could only say that her son Johnny died for no apparent reason except old age. This happened to others.

"Finally, the police came and arrested him for murder. It never made the press. When they led him out of the house, well, he looked like he was a fifty-five-year-old man. It turns out he was not actually stealing their youth or their time. He was buying it with his money," Agnes explained.

Finishing my iced tea, I shook my head and whispered, "Unbelievable, just unbelievable; and what happened after that?"

"No one knows. Phillip Dugas just disappeared. He knew too much history. As they say, he knew where all the bodies were buried," she concluded.

Another secret of New Orleans is encapsulated in the nonprinted verbal sheets of New Orleans time.

After a hug and goodbye, I walked down the porch steps and waved.

Agnes Columbo, my now-gone buddy's mom, admonished, "Teddy, don't trade your time for money. It is the most precious thing you have."

Buster and George, a Trilogy:

Part I: A Beautiful Spring Day

The early spring afternoon sun cast a pleasing shadow on the back of my old friend George and his springer spaniel, Buster. Unlike the summer sun, which can be hard on the eyes, this spring sunshine was light and crisp. George could not see me as I approached him from behind. He sat on a bench and watched the golfers tee off on the Painted Hills golf course. Buster sat, too. No leash. He, like George, was in the winter of his life. No energy to chase squirrels or the recent spring robin, which hopped in front of them. Buster had patches of gray mingled with his white and black patches. George, like Buster, had a head of gray hair and a day or two's gray beard growth. Their appearance revealed that they were seasoned veterans of life. They both lost the people who cared for them. Now they had each other.

Boom, another golfer teed off.

George often told me stories of working at the Pabst Brewery as a young fellow. His job was to watch the bottles pass while looking for intruders such as mice or insects. He wore special glasses for the job. The bottles eventually stopped passing; the Brewery was sold and later shut down. Like so many other Kansas industrial workers, his pension and health benefits were also lost.

"There was a time anyone with a high school degree could get a job at some factory and raise a family in Kansas," he told me a week ago.

Rounding the bench, I caught Buster and George's attention

"Hey, Buster," George's raspy voice spoke. "Look who is here. It's Garbo. Grab a seat and watch these guys tee off."

Swat-pop, another tee shot.

"HI, George. What ya, say Buster?" I blurted as I sat and petted Buster's head.

He licked my hand; his eyelids hid his big brown eyes staring up at me. His swishy tail beat a rhythm.

Buster was more than a solution George's son picked up from the Humane Society a few years after he lost his wife. He was a lifeline. After fifty-six years of marriage, George found himself by himself at the age of eighty-four. She was his oasis in the storms of life. Crushing loneliness was placed upon a mental capacity and spirit worn out with age. Buster's owner, a nice older lady, died, and, despite Buster's age, he was put up for adoption. George picked him. They have been buddies for three years.

Swish-click, a tee shot off the mark. We caught the golfer's lament: "Oh no darn it!"

Soon some women tee off. They are not happy with their shot. Their bright clothes complement their athletic golf swing. As she slams her club down in disgust, Buster starts to bark.

"Easy, Buster. Garbo, Buster is a ladies' man, just like me. Those women can really drive the ball. Have you seen how far they hit it on the Golf Channel? They have a poetry to their movement. Don't you agree, Buster?" George asked.

Buster looked up and shuffled his feet in agreement.

"Well, Garbo. Time for us to head home; we've got a nap waiting for us. Hope to see you again here sometime this weekend," George said as he shook my hand.

"Sounds good. See ya, George. Bye, Buster. Be a good dog, don't cause George any trouble," I said.

Just as the warm spring sun reflected off their gray hair, they cast a warm violet shadow as they left me. I leaned back on the bench. It was a beautiful spring day.

Tall Short Stories from the Comedic Mind of Garbo

Part II: Summer Blue Skies

The cicada bugs beat out a steady shrill of sound, announcing to anyone who wasn't paying attention that summer heat had arrived. Not the usual Kansas heat of 95 degrees, which brings out lots of complaining from the heartland faithful who want a perfect 76 degrees. Some days we reached 100 degrees. Surely George and Buster are missing today. I asked the employee in the Painted Hills Golf pro shop if he had seen them.

"They are sitting on the bench at the fifteenth green watching the early risers come in," he chuckled.

Sure enough. From a short distance, the fifteenth putting green appeared like a giant tablecloth, perfectly manicured and rolled, displaying subtle hills and valleys made of a soft, flat yellow-green grass contrasted by the deep green rough surrounding it. If all of humanity disappeared and Martians landed on the green, what would they think of such a strange sight? Perhaps they'd see the white flag on a pole in the middle of the green, with the number "15" on it, and think it was some secret code or country.

"Hey, Buster. Look who is here? Garbo! Come over here, Garbo. Grab a cold bottled water and watch. The pin placement is a killer," announced George.

Walking up to the bench, I petted Buster's head, then shook George's hand. Buster tried to jump up, but his old hips wouldn't let him. I bent down and laughed, pet his shaggy head, and scratched behind his long ears. That always made him shake his head while his ears rotated back and forth like a big fury fan.

"Good boy, Buster. Hi, George. Good to see you. Got room on the bench for an old guy?" I elbowed.

"Old guy? Why you are a spring chicken compared to this raggedy old dog and me. Come on, Buster, move down and make room," George commanded with a smile.

For Buster, it was Maisy. She got the springer spaniel as a puppy. His black and white silky hair hid his big puppy feet as he stumbled to retrieve everything Maisy could throw. Years would go by, and a backyard full of memories ended when Maisy came home with a tumor diagnosis. Before she died, she arranged with the Humane Society to care for Buster. Loyal Buster was at her side during the final hospice visits at home. The nurses took him into his backyard for the last time. His many chew toys, balls, rubber bones, and rubber rings on ropes all lay scattered. A sign of good times with Maisy, now no more. They say dogs deeply sense a loss. A few days later, George, a recent widower, found Buster at the Humane Society.

"Garbo, one guy four-putted! His friends told him he should take up lawn bowling, and they then told him he lost twenty bucks!" George laughed as he pounded his cane for emphasis while his half-covered steel blue eyes sparkled in the shade.

"George, that is why I don't play this silly game. And besides, you gotta be nuts to play in this heat," I commented.

Buster began to slurp up the water George poured into a bowl. The golfers walked by. One told us he was giving up the game. Another petted Buster's head. Buster stopped drinking and suddenly jumped up and licked the fellow's hand, getting him all wet.

"Hey, Buster. Get down," George called out. "He hasn't jumped up in a long time. He must really like you."

"He feels sorry for me after my terrible putting. I'll take any affection I can get," sighed the golfer.

Walking away, the final golfer who played so poorly remarked about how their wives make them play to get out of the house, no matter how hot it is.

"I wish I had my wife to tell me what to do," George spoke to the hot air surrounding us. "So, Garbo, there was this guy who was about to make a putt and, on the road next to the course, a hearse goes by. The guy takes off his hat, bows his head, then puts on the cap and makes the putt. His buddies ask him what that was all about. The golfer replies, 'For thirty-five years, she was a great wife!'"

Sweat dripped into my laugh lines and began to burn my eyes. "Ha! Ahh, good one, George!" I laughed.

I always had a joke for George. Today the heat made my quick wit go numb. We sat quietly and watched as another white ball hit the green.

Tall Short Stories from the Comedic Mind of Garbo

Part III: A Fall to Remember

People from all over the country make trips to Kansas in the fall. Our treasured trees begin the process of going to sleep for the winter. On the Painted Hills golf course, the leaves begin to change into such amazing subtle colors. Red, orange, yellow—not really but some intensely pleasing color with a blend of those shades. Like a symphony of changing color, each tree changes and drops its leaves at the right time—the time the ancient days determined millenniums ago.

It was my usual Wednesday, time to give George and Buster a hard time. Walking into the pro shop, I greeted the pro and asked where George and Buster were today.

"Check the eighteenth green. I think I saw Buster by the bench," said Sam, the pro.

The eighteenth hole was a bit of a walk. It was the final hole and had the most challenging green. From a distance, I noticed Buster sitting on the bench next to a big grocery bag and someone besides George with him.

"Hi, Buster," I shouted as I approached within ten feet of the bench.

Buster barked. All dogs bark. Some barks are friendly; some are a warning. This bark was different. How would I describe a bark with a trailing emotion at the end? I think I just did!

"Hi, you must be Garbo," a tall fiftysomething fellow announced with his hand extended.

"Yes, I am," I said, slightly confused.

"I am George's son, Ed," he said and began to choke his next words out. "My dad had a stroke five days ago, and yesterday, he left us."

The words tore at me. Some words have a built-in sadness that you hope you never hear. For once, I had no retort, no funny line, nothing. I just stared first at Ed, then Buster.

"I don't know what to say. I am glad to meet you, but I am sorry for your loss," I said. "Wow, can't believe it." I continued murmuring while looking safely at my shoes.

Our conversation continued for a few moments—the usual "he had a full life, he was a great guy, what a sense of humor, he is in a better place with his wife"—words that quench a conversational void, a sadness for a while, then a few hours later, it returns. These are our God moments. They define us as humans and make us a little higher than the angels.

"Garbo, George always spoke about his good times with you and had a final request. Old Buster needs a new home," Ed said with a smile while petting Buster's head. "My dad asked to see if you might provide a home for him."

"You mean this Buster—the one who likes to sit on the bench and watch putters miss their putts?" I blurted out over the lump in my throat. "Does he eat much and need special attention? Because I am a busy guy."

Buster barked and jumped off the bench. He began to rummage through the bag that rested on the ground. Out came a rope with a ball on the end. Ed watched while Buster pushed it into my hand only to pull it out and shake it. I grabbed it and gave him a good tug-of-war.

Taking Buster by the leash, I asked Ed if he was free to watch the golfers next Wednesday at 4 p.m. with Buster and me.

"Sounds good," answered Ed

"See you next week," I waved.

Stopping a few steps away, I turned and said, "Oh, one more thing, Ed."

"What's that? He asked.

"You have to come with some jokes, and they have to be funny like your dad's," I demanded as Buster barked.

"You got it!" Ed smiled.

"See you next week," I waved. "Come on, Buster. I need a guard dog, and you have to earn your keep."

Buster and I turned and left. I took a deep breath of the crisp fall air as we crunched the beautiful leaves on our pathway home.

Clouds on Bellano Court

Remember when you were four or five or eleven or twelve? Of course not, but I can tell you that you laid down on the grass and looked at the sky. Every kid does. My grandkids do too. You stared with amazement at the clouds. Just you and the clouds floating softly in a weightless blue sky. You achieved a bond, a bond that became an invisible wall. Nothing was going to penetrate and distract you from that heartfelt connection. You became delightful.

Beautiful clouds against a blue background have frustrated

painters for generations. Blue paint just doesn't do it. There is depth, there are tones and values of ever-changing blue. Simple magic. Simple genius. The soft cloud is so light yet so heavy that it can cause a shadow on the ground or on the waves of the ocean. The belly of the cloud has shadows: yellow, light-glowing yellow, orange, pink, gray, light gray, and finally, dirty gray. Where are those colors coming from?

Why is it that when you were a kid, you got great pleasure from looking at the sky and the clouds? Maybe you were eating a popsicle at the time. You had no job to think about, no girlfriend or boyfriend, no car payments or mortgage to worry about.

Your relationships were uncomplicated.

"We are playing baseball; do you want to play? No? Okay."

Rejection passed as those clouds slowly rotated and moved across the sky. You were glad.

Nothing was left in the bucket to make you upset or distract you from that big floating cloud. The edges looked like white cotton candy. They actually moved and curled up. What happens if one cloud crashes into another? I guess that won't happen because the invisible wind is moving both of them. A stream of unseen, invisible wind. How much does the wind weigh?

No charge card bill to think about. Just big puffy clouds.

No son going through a nonstop messy divorce or son-in-law facing back surgery. No parent is about to enter a nursing home.

Just giant cotton balls rotating slowly in the wind with gray, pink bottoms. This one looks like the shape of our car. Here comes a rabbit.

No daughter who consistently picks the wrong kind of men. No grandchildren being raised in an uncommon manner.

No surprise diagnosis from your doctor. No note from your wife saying after all these years, she has found someone else. No messages from the mirror you look at daily.

You surrendered all to those chalk-like baked potatoes way above you. Your restless legs twitched. That cloud looks like a swan.

Overbearing supervisors did not come to mind, nor did colleagues at work who routinely irritate you. Just that swirl of white surrounded by intense blue, but not just blue. Blue-blue is described by words that betray the description—thalo blue, cerulean blue, robin's egg blue, violet-blue. Above the clouds are one color, below the clouds another. How can that be? Do these clouds divide the sky into two?

Everything dissolved away, and a certain contentment showed up in that tiny pre-teen heart of yours. You were happy. You seized the moment, and the moment was solely yours. Heart, mind, and soul were amused.

Those human tragedy things listed above were there for you to possibly, eventually face. They were waiting for you. Try as you must, they could not be avoided. You do not have full control of your destiny. Today, new ones lie in wait for you. Is this your chance to empty the bucket and just feel the grass and watch the sky show—to create that invisible wall that keeps everything out while you embrace the movement of the clouds? Perhaps your legs will still twitch.

Perhaps it is time to again lay in the grass, eat a popsicle, and watch the clouds go by. To reach back to that simple time and become that child again. Blue sky pierced by white, yellow, pink, orange-colored clouds. See those clouds as exclamation points to the good, the noble, the tomorrows, which will be a better day.

May that peace be yours.

Garbo

Acknowledgments

Special thanks to the following, without whose encouragement and laughter, this book would not be in your hands: Patty, Nancy, Gini, Sarah, Kari, Leslie, Ian, Paul, Bill, Lucy, Nazar, Peter, Uncle Hach, Aunt Mary, Dave and Eddi, Levon, Stacy, Auntie Cathy, Merrijo, Lydia, and many more who took the time to be my friend. Finally, my love and partner on this blue-green marble, my soulmate, my reason to wake up each day, my wife, Mary Kay.

About the Author

I was born in Milwaukee, Wisconsin, to first-generation Armenian American parents. As a child, I heard my grandparents and those around them tell stories. Armenians are great storytellers. We will talk to anyone who listens or who we think might be listening. Strangers in elevators are our best targets. If you are like that, you probably have an Armenian ancestor. We have sad stories, stories with life lessons, funny stories, and stories we think are funny. I have told them a hundred times. And before me, generations have told them. Nobody bothered to write them down. Who had the time? Where can you find a pen that writes nowadays? Finally, they are written down for your enjoyment.

I am a retired dentist who has written several books. Not true. I thought about writing them. I just haven't written them down because it is easier to talk, and you don't need spell check. I did write the book about an amazing yellow Lab named Sandy called *Sandy and Garbo* (used copies on Amazon). I perform stand-up comedy for fundraisers—people pay me to stop with the jokes! Dentists need lots of jokes. I am available for parties. For the comedy. Although retired, I never lost my love of people and their unique stories.

Made in the USA
Columbia, SC
09 November 2022